Sticky
Fingers

Sticky Fingers

Sticky Fingers

Niki Burnham

Simon Pulse
New York   London   Toronto   Sydney

This book is a work of fiction. Any references to historical events, real people, or real locales are used fictitiously. Other names, characters, places, and incidents are the product of the author's imagination, and any resemblance to actual events or locales or persons, living or dead, is entirely coincidental.

SIMON PULSE
An imprint of Simon & Schuster Children's Publishing Division
1230 Avenue of the Americas, New York, NY 10020
Text copyright © 2005 by Nicole Burnham
All rights reserved, including the right of reproduction in whole or in part in any form.
SIMON PULSE and colophon are registered trademarks of Simon & Schuster, Inc.
Designed by Ann Zeak
The text of this book was set in Garamond 3.
Manufactured in the United States of America
First Simon Pulse edition September 2005
10 9 8 7 6 5 4 3 2 1
Library of Congress Control Number 2004109060
ISBN 0-689-87649-1

For my fantabulous brother, Joe,
who might actually read this one.
Thanks for the push and all that.

Chapter

1

"It's a thin envelope, Courtney," I say. A white #10 envelope bearing a Cambridge, Massachusetts, return address. "I nearly flipped past it when I was sorting through the Christmas cards and catalogs. Gotta be bad news."

Everyone knows acceptance letters arrive in oversize envelopes crammed with info about housing and registration.

"Chill, Jenna." The sound of a Coke being slurped comes over the phone line. It's one of those Courtney Delahunt habits that irritate the hell out of most people, but that I learned to tune out years and years ago. I hear the clatter of the can hitting her desk before she says, "Take a deep breath, say a prayer to the gods of Early Action admissions, and then read the damned thing already. I don't know why you didn't just rip it open the second you pulled it out of the mailbox."

Because I don't want to see that ugly "We regret to inform you . . ." sentence in black and white, that's why. Don't want to go through applying Regular Action to a dozen different schools and dealing with all the forms and essays and self-promoting fakery. Not to mention paying a couple nights' baby-sitting income—*each*—for the application fees.

And maybe not getting into my first-choice school even then.

"I think I should wait for my parents." It's a totally lame excuse, but technically they're just as invested in the whole process as I am. Mom spent hours reading over my essays, critiquing them, then reading them again before I mailed out my application a couple months ago. And Dad said he'd put off buying a (desperately needed) new car for himself if I manage to get into an Ivy, just so I won't have to take out any more student loans than absolutely necessary.

"And I think you're just being chicken because this means everything to you," Courtney argues right back. "Your parents would *want* you to look. Mateus the Great agrees with me."

"Mat's over there?" I frown, flipping the envelope over and holding it up under the kitchen's tacky 1980s track lights. Maybe I can see through it if I get it at the right angle. It'll probably be less painful if I get a hint of what the letter says and then open it for real.

"He doesn't have to work until five today. And it's my day off."

There's a scuffling noise, and then Mat's lightly accented voice cuts in. "And we have the house to ourselves until then, okay? Her parents have a company Christmas party or something in downtown Boston. So open the envelope and give us the news, Jenna. Courtney and I don't have much time to celebrate, know what I'm saying?"

I hear some clicks, then Courtney pops back on the line, meaning she grabbed a cordless from another room. She makes an exasperated sound I presume is directed at Mat for stealing the first phone right out of her hand, then says, "Seriously, Jenna. I bet you got in. And if you didn't, no biggie. You know you'll get in during the regular cycle if you reapply. Your SAT scores freaking rocked. Your grades are great, and Hemingway could've written your admission essays—"

"I get it already."

"Come on, Jenna." Mat's voice is softer this time, more understanding, his South American accent more pronounced. "Otherwise, you're going to drive yourself crazy for the next few hours, and I'll go crazy at work tonight wondering what your letter said."

For a brief moment, I envy Courtney. How easy would life be if I were as laid back as Courtney about school stuff, and if I had a Brazilian boyfriend as gorgeous and understanding as Mat?

Of course, I do have a gorgeous and understanding boyfriend. Scott might not have Mat's accent, but he has other assets.

Lots of other assets.

"Okay," I say, trying not to sigh out loud. "Send me good vibes."

"Vibes a' comin'," Courtney says. "Now rip that sucker open!"

Cradling the phone between my shoulder and ear, I open the kitchen utility drawer, find the letter opener my parents use for the bills, then slit the top seam of the envelope, careful not to catch the letter inside with the tip of the opener.

I close my eyes, pull out the page, then flatten it against the yellow Formica countertop and make one last wish.

"Read it aloud," Courtney says.

I take a deep breath, trying to slow down my pounding heartbeat, then open my eyes to focus on the black type. "It says, 'Dear Ms. Kassarian, we are pleased to inform you that—'"

"You got in!" Courtney's yell nearly renders me deaf. "'Pleased to inform' is always good news!"

"I knew it. ¡Parabéns!" Mat explains that this is Brazilian Portuguese for "congrats," then adds, "No way were you getting rejected."

I keep reading aloud, trying to ignore them long enough to get this through my head. "'. . . you have been accepted into the freshman class for the upcoming academic year as part of the Harvard Early Action admissions program.' Oh, wow." I stare at the single sheet of paper, hardly believing the words on the page. Or the logo at the top.

"'Oh, wow' is right!" Courtney says. "I mean, this changes your whole life. And your parents are going to be *thrilled*."

"Them? What about me? I was so sure when I saw the envelope that it was going to be a serious smackdown. But it says that they'll mail more information in April, including financial aid applications, housing forms, and a guide to undergraduate activities." The whole "guide to undergraduate activities" is hysterical, since I know they're trying to make the fact they don't have fraternities and sororities look okay.

Of course, Mat and Courtney probably don't know that's what it really means, and I'm not going to clarify. Courtney's dying to do the sorority pledge thing next year, but me, well, I'd rather chew on broken glass.

I read through the whole letter again, not even hearing what Courtney and Mat are saying on the other end of the line. Tears start rolling down my cheeks as reality sets in, and I don't care.

This is the best Christmas present ever.

All those evenings I skipped going to movies—even the ones I was dying to see—or made excuses to not go out with Courtney, Scott, Mat, and all our other friends. All the times I came straight home after volleyball practice or tennis without stopping to have pizza or hang out with my friends, just so I'd have an extra hour to study or to check over a project one last time.

All the nights I left Scott's house early, despite the fact that every fiber of my being ached to stay just so I could feel his arms around me for one more minute, or so I could kiss him one more time.

I stare down at the letter and smile to myself. Courtney's right: This changes my whole life. In just eight months I'll be going to Harvard, and even better, so will Scott. Because if I managed to get in, he definitely did. He's always done a smidge better than me at everything, so getting into Harvard is practically guaranteed now.

Maybe on our first day he'll pull me over to the

library stairs and give me a mind-bending kiss, just like the one he gave me for luck when we went for our tour. And this time, it'll be because we're celebrating that the sacrifice paid off for both of us.

"Jenna? You're awfully quiet. You okay?"

"Oh, yeah. Definitely yeah." And then I let out a shriek meant to render Courtney deaf.

"Hey, how was Stop & Shop today? Lots of fun and excitement?" I try my best to sound casual, but I know I don't. I've been dying for the last four hours, waiting for Scott to get home from working the cash register, ringing up artichokes and Tuna Helper for grouchy customers who don't give a rip that he's going to be leaving it all for freaking Harvard in a few months.

"Tons of fun," he says, his tone dry and sarcastic. "Someone actually bought okra. It was the highlight of my entire day. Seriously, what do people do with okra? But I know you're dying to ask about my mail. What was in yours?"

"I have an envelope in my hand right this minute. White with a crimson logo for the return address."

"Me too. I read it outside, standing in the snow by the mailbox. The wind nearly blew it out of my hand, but I couldn't wait. Was yours thick or thin?"

"Thin."

"Mine too," he says.

I grin, then wrap my finger through a stray chunk of mud-brown hair that's fallen into my face and loop it back over my ear. He got in and now he's teasing me. Jerk.

If I hadn't gotten in too, I think I might be offended.

"Totally blows," he adds, and I freeze at his tone of voice. "At least I have the applications for Brown, Cornell, and B.C. almost ready to go. And I told you I decided to go ahead and apply to UMass, didn't I? I mean, Harvard's still my focus, but whatta pain in the ass. I'm going to be using every obscenity in the book while I'm filling all that stuff out again."

"So . . . you're saying you didn't get in?" Part of me wants to think he's kidding, but I can tell from all his false bravado that he's so *not*.

"Nope. You know, I didn't realize until I got that damned letter how much I'd been counting on it.

But now that I've had a few minutes to absorb it, I'm not that worried. The rejection was a form letter, but one of the *good* form letters, you know? They encouraged me to apply Regular Action and said my chances of getting in are high, that I'm a very strong candidate, yadda yadda yadda."

I stare at the wall, trying to process what Scott's saying. The guy practically maxed out the SAT. Plus, he's in AP everything, has fantastic grades, *and* he's a total jock. Harvard couldn't want a more perfect applicant. How could he not have gotten in?

And how in the world had *I*?

"Jennn-na? Earth to Jenna Kassarian? What'd yours say? Same thing, I bet, that you're a strong candidate. There's no way you got the total rejection form letter."

I take a deep breath, trying to figure out how I can tell him. Scott's totally cool about most things. We don't really compete with each other—only in a good-natured, push-each-other-to-do-better kind of way—because we both have the type of personality where we're very competitive with ourselves. And thankfully, he's not one of those guys who feels inadequate if his girlfriend gets a better grade than he does or beats him at sports or video games or whatever. He's happy as long as he did the best he could.

But I have a niggling feeling he's not going to take this well. Not on the inside.

"Holy shit. You got in, didn't you?" He sounds quiet, and I wonder if he's annoyed, but then he says, "Jenna! Tell me you got in!" And it's total excitement.

"Yeah, I did," I manage, even though I hate to tell him this way, after he didn't and I know he's really bummed about it.

"Jen, that's terrific!" He *sounds* happy for me. Genuinely happy. I know that's good . . . but somehow, his happiness makes me feel even worse.

"Thanks. I'm kind of shocked. Actually, there's no 'kind of'—I'm completely shocked. When I saw I got in, I was positive you had too. Your grades are as good as mine, and your SAT scores were way better—"

"It's more than scores, and you know it. Your essays rocked, and our extracurriculars are different. Mine are all sports, but you've got sports and student council. And that brainiac literary magazine you did freshman and sophomore year."

True. But hearing him rationalize it doesn't make me feel any better. I flop backward on my bed, sinking into the pillows, then pull the acceptance letter out of the envelope.

"But it's still wrong. You deserve to be there. And I want you there with *me*." I finger the expensive stationery and mentally curse the admissions gurus for not giving Scott's application a better look. Because if they had, he'd be in.

"I'll be there, Jenna. Really. It's just not official yet."

"Even if you get in somewhere else? What if you get a scholarship to Cornell or something?" Everything I've envisioned about next year includes Scott.

Maybe I should send out a few more applications. I don't have to commit to Harvard until May 1, so there's nothing that says I can't—

I close my eyes, dropping the letter and grinding my fist against my forehead.

How stupid is this making me? I don't want to go anywhere else. Never have. This has always been my dream, and now it's getting all screwed up.

"Harvard's still my first choice, and now I have even more reason to want to go there," Scott says.

"We're going to be together." He hesitates, then asks, "So what are you doing right now?"

"Theoretically? Studying for next week's advanced biology midterm." Even though I don't have to. I've already studied a ton.

"In reality?"

"Wigging out over the letter. Both letters."

"Me too," he admits. "I have calc homework to do, but I can't focus. So do you want to go out?"

I glance at the bright red digital numbers on my clock radio. Nearly eight p.m. "On a Tuesday?"

"How often do you have something like this to celebrate? I think it'd be wrong not to go out. Neither of us is getting much done, anyway."

I probably would be productive, eventually. I'm one of those insane people who could lose an arm in the middle of an exam and still finish it if it meant the difference between getting an A-minus and an A.

"It's freezing out," I argue. And I tell him I think it's supposed to snow again later.

"So what? The roads were fine when I was coming home from work. And I bought something for you, anyway."

"You did? What?"

"We knew the letters were coming either today or tomorrow. No matter what they said, I figured you deserved flowers."

It's official. I have the best boyfriend in the world. "Scott, you know you didn't have to—"

"I wanted to. And I want to celebrate now. I'll be there in half an hour."

My knee-jerk reaction is to argue some more. It's the 1950s throwback fuddy-duddy in me. Which is, coincidentally, the part of me that's also responsible for my totally bent studying habits. But instead, I fold the paper, slide it into my nightstand drawer, and say, "Perfect."

Just for this one night.

I close my eyes and lean back against the soft headrest of Scott's passenger seat, then extend my hands toward the dash so they'll be close to the heat vents.

Most guys' cars smell stale. Discarded french fries and mysterious sticky spills meet your fingers whenever you go to buckle your seat belt, and if someone sitting in the backseat claims that there are mushrooms growing in the dark areas beneath the seats, no one looks surprised. But not in Scott's car. He keeps his bright red Jetta pristine.

It's been a year and a half since his dad and his stepmother, Amber, surprised him with it on his sixteenth, and I still can't get over it. (Of course, neither can Scott's mom, who wasn't consulted until it was already parked in her driveway with a big white bow on top.) It sure beats my old Corolla—a puke-green car my parents bought when I was in preschool—any day of the week. But if I get to ride in Scott's Jetta anytime I want, with the most gorgeous male in all of Massachusetts sitting beside me, of course, then who am I to have car envy?

"Where to? Bennigan's?" he asks. "Or there's the John Harvard's at Shoppers World. Might be more appropriate, given our day."

"Doesn't matter to me." Anywhere in Framingham would suit me fine. I just need to clear my brain. And to make sure Scott's really okay with everything. "Frankly, I like just being in the car right now. It's peaceful."

"Trade it straight across for your car and your letter," he says, not even missing a beat.

Oh, crap. I crack an eyelid and look sideways at him to see if he's serious. Thankfully, he's smiling. "You know you should have gotten in before me," I tell him again. I have that walking-on-eggshells sensation, which I've never had with him before. And probably shouldn't have now, but I do. I hate feeling so happy and so guilty at the same time.

"So make it up to me after dinner."

I reach past the emergency brake and rest my hand—now that the warm air has jump-started my circulation—on his thigh as he turns the car onto Route 9, heading toward Shoppers World. He puts his hand over mine, sliding my fingers a few inches higher. Not into terribly dangerous territory, but enough to make my insides do a little dance. And enough for me to know he doesn't want me to spend tonight moping about his letter.

We pull up to a stoplight, and he leans over and gives me the most delicious kiss.

I absolutely cannot go without him all year next year. No way.

"You know what else your letter means, right?" he asks between kisses. "That you can relax now. Stop worrying so much about how your future might hinge on spending an extra ten minutes getting a calc problem right, or on kissing up to teachers for good recommendation letters. You can start going out more, living it up. Seeing more of me."

"Mmm. Light's green." I straighten up in the seat but leave my hand exactly where he positioned it. I love how guys' legs are just rock hard, how you can feel their muscles right through their jeans.

"I mean it, Jen. Your grades won't go into the toilet if you let yourself have a little fun." He puts his foot on the gas as the station wagon in front of us starts to move. "If you're ever going to get out and party, now's the time. Take advantage."

I smile at him but don't say anything. It isn't that simple. I'm probably going to be class salutatorian, since Scott has the valedictorian slot totally locked up—well, if I nail advanced bio—and if not, then I'll graduate ranked third or fourth. If I kick back, though, if I go out and party and spend all my free time with Scott, will that class rank I've killed myself to maintain go right out the window?

Then again, maybe it doesn't matter anymore, now that I'm not trying to impress a board of (presumably) old white guys sitting around an admissions table in a red brick building in Cambridge.

As if he can read my mind, Scott says, "You just can't let go, can you?"

"I can." Maybe. "I mean, I'm out tonight, and you know how neurotic I am about weeknights."

"Really?" His tone is sarcastic, but he's grinning at me.

"It's easier for you," I say. "You cram for fifteen minutes in the hallway before a class, then go in and ace the exam. Every single time. I've never been that way." This shouldn't be a news flash to him. He knows I have to work way harder to get good grades than he does.

"Doesn't mean you can't loosen up a little now, though." His voice is flirty as he adds, "Otherwise, when will you?"

"I don't know. But I'm not sure I know how to loosen up at this point. I mean, what if I can't get *un*–laid back again?"

And how far is too far, anyway? If I go nuts at a party once? Or once a week? At what point do my grades start to slide, or worse, my attitude? It's all about inertia. And I really do want to make salutatorian. And do well in the spring science fair. And kick ass at Harvard next year. And, and, and.

I would never admit it aloud, even to Scott, but I like me the way I am. Driven. Busting my ass to do everything just the right way makes me feel good about myself. Bulletproof.

He raises an eyebrow at me and gives me this totally sexy look that's full of promise. "But?"

"But . . . you do make it damned tempting." Okay, it's not exactly what I was thinking, but it isn't a total lie, either. The guy has brains—which is definitely my top boyfriend requirement—and he also has, in Courtney-speak, a yum factor that's off the scale. Which is probably why I still freak out just a little bit every time he kisses me, or whenever he gives me one of his *I know what you're thinking* looks from across the room in Economics, even though we've been together for a year now. Deep in my gut, I still feel like Scott's too good for me. Not because he's more popular, necessarily—I'm in that social strata that's below superpopular, but I'm not a nobody, either. It's more that he's smarter, better looking, more athletic, more everything than I am. He has that wavy brown hair you always see on actors and male models, and his eyes are a misty green, the kind everyone comments on. But best of all is his face. It's flat-out perfect. Everything's in the right proportion, and his skin is smooth and clear and just dark enough to look slightly tan and outdoorsy year-round.

It's just wrong for someone who looks the way he does to also be at the top of our class, and to *also* be superathletic.

And someday I'm afraid he's going to figure out that he's a perfect male who can get anyone he wants, and he'll tell me buh-bye.

It's not paranoia. Just enough of a gut feeling to make me grateful for what I've got and to keep me on my toes. It's not low self-esteem, either. (Total pet peeve: I hate when counselors and teachers blame everything on low self-esteem in teens. Some of us actually have self-esteem, believe it or not. And when we make mistakes, it's not because of a defect in our psyche. We screw up just because.)

The whole thing with Scott is just knowing myself and who I am. I don't blow tons of money on the latest clothes, like Courtney does, just so I can look fantastic every hour of every day. All my studying has given me an ass that's a size or so bigger than what I'd have in an ideal world, and even though tennis and volleyball help, I know I'm going to get the rumored freshman fifteen next year if I don't, well, watch my ass.

And there's my obsession with grades. Most people don't get it. Well, Scott sorta does and sorta doesn't. He expects good grades, whereas I'm simply terrified of getting a bad one.

But that's all okay. It's all about knowing what I want, what my limitations are, and then being happy with who I am. Which is why I wonder where my limitations are in the way of letting loose and partying.

Scott takes one hand off the wheel and laces his fingers through mine. He keeps his eyes on the road as he slows down in the John Harvard's lot, looking for a spot. "Seriously, Jenna. Try to relax and be happy. Just for tonight?"

"Okay, I think I can handle one night." I give him a lopsided grin that's meant to make him feel better, even though I want to scream, *I'd be more relaxed if everyone would stop friggin' telling me to relax!* Even my parents didn't think I did a sufficient happy dance over the letter—and I actually went out to the garage to show them when they came home from work because I couldn't wait until they got inside. They both thought I should have called them at work.

Scott sees a spot a row over and lets go of my hand. Once he's nabbed it, I start to unbuckle my seat belt, but realize he hasn't pulled his keys out of the ignition. "What?"

"How hungry are you?"

I shrug, wondering where this is going, even though I suspect from the glimmer in his eyes. "Not very. I ate dinner at six. I just figured we'd sit and have sodas and dessert or something. Maybe dis the idiots at Harvard for sending you the wrong letter."

"I have a better idea."

He shifts the car into reverse, looks at me for confirmation that I'm truly not about to die of starvation, then drives out of the lot.

I don't even have to ask where he's going. "Our" nursery is only a mile or two down Speen Street. In the summer, flowering trees and plants on wooden pallets cram the huge parking lot behind the greenhouses, waiting for suburbanites to spend exorbitant amounts of money to take them home (and probably kill them, anyway). But now, in the dead of winter, only skater kids show up to use the lot—and then only if there's not a thick layer of ice and snow on the ground, like there is tonight.

Even though it's not glamorous, it's the one place we know we can always have total privacy. And one of these nights, it just might become the place where I lose my virginity. Not *tonight,* but someday. For now, though, it's the perfect escape from reality for both of us.

Chapter
2

"Scott, let's slow down, okay?" I whisper to him for the second time in as many minutes.

Thanks to the cold outside and the heater blasting inside, steam has built up on the Jetta windows so thick that I can reach over and write my name on the glass if I want. Just like in a movie. And Scott is kissing me but good—enough to make me want to yank my jeans off and finally, um, *relax,* right here and now. It's completely and totally romantic.

But somehow, movie-like setting and all, it just doesn't feel right. Well, not right for *that.*

"Aren't you having fun?" he teases, easing his fingers just low enough to make me squirm. Man, he's good at knowing just where to put them.

"You know I am. But let's not, not here." Does he not realize it's a Tuesday? And late? And that we're in a freaking Jetta in a snowy parking lot where the Framingham cops can come up at any second and start knocking on the windows with their flashlights? (And they will if they see the car parked here, where a car really has no business being.)

Okay, maybe he does know all this, and that's the attraction, which I do understand.

Hoooo boy, do I understand.

But somewhere, deep in the back of my brain, a little alarm is going off, telling me that I'll regret it if I don't tell him to stop. *Now.* No matter how incredible it feels.

"I don't think it's going to get better than here," he mumbles, but he stops unbuttoning my jeans and pushes up on his elbows anyway.

We have the passenger seat reclined all the way back, and he's lying on top of me. We can manage this as long as we both have our coats off, so they're stuffed in the backseat with my sweater tossed on top. I have his favorite black henley pushed up to his shoulders, so I can feel his flat, firm stomach against my not-so-firm one. It's completely wonderful, lying here with him, letting my fingers run all over his warm body and breathing in the smell of him. But the semi-pissed-off look on his face is making me hate myself for sounding like some prude housewife with a headache.

Especially because I really do love Scott, and I love our clandestine little make-out spot. And as uptight as I can be about school and grades and stuff, I'm not all that uptight about the whole sex thing. "Look, Scott—"

"You don't want your first time to be in a car."

"Exactly."

I hate having to say no, especially because this isn't the first time I've said it. And I hate it even worse because on the five or six occasions when we've discussed whether we want to take that next step— and danced around the whole virginity thing—he's never once said a word about not wanting *his* first time to be in a car.

I did ask him straight out once. He just grinned and gave me this little *well, you know* kind of shrug. And then he changed the subject. That alone gave me a pretty good answer.

I'll bet fifty bucks he slept with Ashley Hayden. She took him to her junior prom when he was a sophomore, and since I had a blinding crush on him at the time, I know for a fact they stayed out all night. I was paying attention.

And if not Ashley, then Bridget McConley. He went out with her all of sophomore year (when I was first noticing him, and—unfortunately—the fact that he was already taken). He completely and totally adored her. But then she cheated on him with some gorgeous guy from Holliston during a track meet. That's when Scott decided to dump Bridget—despite her dramatic, crying apologies, and despite how loopy lovey he was over her—and hook up with Ashley when she needed a prom date to make *her* ex jealous. It was a total revenge thing, he told me once, on both their parts, and probably a stupid thing to do.

Okay, he definitely slept with Ashley. Bridget

might've had a quickie make-out session with the Holliston Hottie behind the bleachers, but she was way more conservative about the sex stuff than Ashley. Plus, Ashley was a year older than Bridget, and everyone already knew Ashley'd slept with her last boyfriend. Well, her last three boyfriends. (Which I think is icky, but I suppose to each her own.)

Still, I don't want to be the ex he someday describes to his buddies as the girl he screwed in his Jetta, saying something like, "I told you about Jetta Jenna. Remember, the girlfriend I had after the girl I screwed as a revenge thing when Bridget hooked up with the Holliston Hottie?"

Ick.

I don't *think* Scott would ever do that, but still. It has to be special. For both of us. No matter what happens in the future.

"I can get a hotel room," he says. "I've got my credit card with me, and there are a couple places back on Route 9. I think there's—"

"We both need to be home in an hour or so." Wow. Usually he backs right off. We've tried to take things slowly since we started going out last year. But if he's been thinking about getting a hotel room . . .

"I don't want to pressure you, but I think your parents will understand if you're a little late tonight. You know, since you're celebrating getting into Harvard." He runs his hand up under my white T-shirt, then gives me one of his wicked little Scott smiles I know is intended to make me cave in. It worked a few weeks ago, when he convinced me to bail on seventh period (there was a substitute) and go out to a movie to celebrate our one-year anniversary, even though I'd never skipped class before. But this is an entirely different situation.

"Scott, I want our first time to be . . . extraordinary." I reach up to touch his cheek, to make sure he can see my eyes and how serious I am. "Something that's going to blow our minds. We don't want to rush just so we can get home and deal with calculus or advanced bio, you know?"

I want it to be a night where we can just hold each other and talk and do it again and again if we want. Like it's supposed to be.

And I definitely don't want to be doing the deed while my head's screwed up with guilt because I got into Harvard and he's stuck waiting months to find out. Even if he does seem like he's okay with the whole thing.

"You're killing me, Jen. I want you so bad, and we've waited forever." His hand starts doing some very interesting things under my shirt, and he lets more of his weight rest on me as he kisses the spot just in front of my ear and whispers, "And you know I can make it special. You know how I feel about you."

"I know," I whisper back. But I wish he'd stop freaking *pushing*. Why don't guys get that pressure takes the special right out of it, no matter how much fun you're having? No matter how much you like them?

His hand slows down. "You said you didn't have a problem with the whole sex-before-marriage thing. It's not me, then, is it?"

I can feel his hipbone rubbing against mine, and he knows I hate that. It hurts. But he doesn't do anything about it, even when I wiggle a little, which kind of pisses me off.

He looks up just enough to catch my eye, and his voice has a teasing tone as he adds, "I bet it's because you got into Harvard and I'm a reject. You're way too good for me now, and you don't know how to tell me."

"Oh, please! One, you're going to get into Harvard, and you know it. And two, as much as I really like your car, this isn't ideal. And neither is a quickie at the Motel 6. That's all there is to it."

He shifts so his hipbone isn't grinding into mine anymore. "Promise?"

He looks so sincere, so *into* me, that I want to say yes—knowing exactly what he's asking me to promise. But how can I promise that, especially when he's being so damned aggressive tonight? Does he expect me to pull out a date book and swear to him that at 4 p.m. next Friday, I'll gladly give him my virginity, provided he supplies us with a great location and no interruptions?

Plus, deep down inside, part of me wonders if he's still trying to prove to himself that he's better than the Holliston Hottie because of the whole Bridget thing. I mean, I don't think that's the case, but I want to be absolutely sure. He did have it pretty bad for her.

"Scott, a 'no' tonight isn't because of you, and it's definitely not because I have a problem with sex."

Well, I don't think I do.

I pull him back down against me, then hook one leg around his waist as best I can in the cramped seat. "And nothing says we can't still have a fabulous time tonight."

That's as good a promise as I can make. At least for now.

"Hey, wait up, Miss Smarty Pants Harvard Girl!"

I spin around at the sound of Courtney's voice. "Shh!" I warn her as she sails out of the library and grabs me on my way to my locker. "Everyone's going to think I'm a total snob if you talk that way."

"You're not a snob. You're just better than the rest of us." She's grinning as she says it, but I'm not. "Oh, come on, Jen, you know I'm kidding. So . . . you notice anything different about me?"

I instantly notice the skirt. Actually, it should be capitalized: The Skirt. It's low-slung denim and cut perfectly for Courtney's figure. It totally shows off her long waist, flat stomach, and (depending on what shirt she wears) her silver belly button ring, but without baring enough skin to break the school dress code. She's been eyeing it over at Natick Mall for weeks. Even made pilgramages to visit it to make sure they hadn't sold out of her size.

"Um, lemme guess," I say, pretending to look down the hall like I'm expecting someone, instead of studying her for whatever's changed. "You forget to put on your eyeliner this morning?"

"Very funny. So whaddya think? Is it not as incredible as I told you it'd be?"

I admit that the skirt looks great—probably the best thing Courtney owns, and that's saying a lot. "I can't believe you blew such a wad of cash, though. You'd better wear it for the next decade."

Courtney's smile goes a little off-kilter, so I quickly add, "When Mat sees it, he's not going to be able to keep his hands off you."

"He already can't." We get to our lockers, and Courtney's smile is back full force. She has her lock open in an instant, then takes a quick glance in the magnetic mirror on the inside of the door so she can inspect her hair. She does this between every single class. It's just her thing. And of course every blond strand is perfectly in place.

"Hey, before I tell you the latest, I have something for you." She pulls a shopping bag out of her locker, then takes out a long black box tied with a white ribbon. As she hands it to me, she says, "For you. For working your tail off so you can follow your dreams. I really admire you for it."

"I can't believe you got me something." I stare at the box, then at Courtney. In most ways, we're total opposites. But ever since she stuck up for me in sixth grade when a bunch of other girls were picking on me, I've respected her for being so incredibly smart about people. And when I repaid her by teaching her how to hold a tennis racket the right way just so she could whack balls against her garage and impress the tennis-playing seventh grader (yes, male) who lived next door to her, it made us inseparable.

We complement each other, I suppose.

"Open it," she says. "Otherwise, I'm going to start belting out 'Wind Beneath My Wings' right here, right now, so everyone in the senior class will know that you're my hero."

"You wouldn't." Although I know she would. I carefully pull the ribbon loose, then set it on my locker shelf so I can save it. Inside the box, there's a thin gold wire necklace with the Chinese symbol for harmony resting on a bed of white tissue paper. My throat instantly gets that tight feeling that makes me hope I'm not going to cry. I mean, this cost her a lot of hours at the Stop & Shop deli counter. Hours she should've been using to pay for her skirt.

"Oh wow, Courtney. How'd you know I wanted this?"

"I saw you hanging out at the jewelry counter while I was drooling over the skirt, so when you weren't looking, I went over and asked the saleslady what you'd been staring at." She shrugs. "Anyway, I decided to get them both. And don't say a word about the money or I'll kill you. You deserve it."

I give Courtney a quick hug. "You know you're the absolute best friend I could ever have. Thank you."

"Put it on."

I set my backpack between my feet, then hook

the necklace under my hair and take a look in Courtney's mirror. "This is beyond beautiful."

"It's perfect on you." Courtney reaches over and adjusts it so the harmony symbol rests flat against my sweater. "But before you gush, I have to tell you what happened yesterday. It's huge."

I frown as I reach into my locker to put my books away from third period. "What?"

"You know how Mat was at my house yesterday when you called with your fantastico news?" Courtney closes her locker, twirls the lock, then leans against the door while she waits for me to finish loading up for my next class.

"Yeah?"

"And my parents weren't?" Her voice is much quieter now, presumably so people at nearby lockers can't hear. Her whole expression is dripping with drama, but since Courtney does this anytime she wants to shock me, I just shove the books into my backpack, then turn and stare at her.

"So?"

"*That* so. We made the most of the opportunity."

I feel my jaw go totally slack. "You didn't."

But it's clear from Courtney's face—her big smile, the fact I can tell she took extra time on her lip gloss and clothes today, and the whole *I'm having a great day and I want everyone to know it* way she's leaning against her locker, with one hand on her hip—that they did.

"He called in sick to work," she explains, still keeping her tone hush-hush. "Told them he had a bad cough and probably shouldn't be behind the counter, but that he'd be happy to come in if they were short."

"And of course they weren't." Hardly any customers hit Mat's Dunkin' Donuts after five. Just cops and firefighters getting ready to work graveyards, or college kids who can't get tables in Starbucks to hang out and do their homework. So being short one employee on a Tuesday night probably isn't a tragedy.

She's dying for me to react, but I haven't the foggiest notion what to say. "Wow, Courtney. I'm, well . . . wow."

"I know. Seriously, there just aren't words." Her smile gets even dopier.

"So, I assume it was, um, good?" I so want the details. And I also don't.

"Beyond good. I can't believe we waited so long, you know? I'll tell you everything when we can get more time to talk, but the bottom line is this: I was stupid to be such a wuss about it."

So long? She and Mat have only been together since September. Maybe even early October. And she hasn't had a boyfriend—not a serious one—before now. Careful to say something that won't be offensive, I tell her, "I don't think you were being a wuss. Maybe you were waiting for a reason."

"Yeah, a dumb reason." She pauses for a second as a couple of girls walk by on their way to their lockers. "Jen, it was in-freaking-credible. I mean, my whole body is still—well, it's like I've taken uppers or something—and I can't get last night out of my head. Neither can Mat. Remember how I told you he said the L word and meant it, like, back on Halloween, when we were at that huge party at Justin DeFoe's house? You know Mat—he wouldn't say something like that unless he means it. And he does, I know he does. And it's just"—she takes this deep, happy breath—"it's beyond anything."

"Courtney, that's—" What? What can I say when

I'm afraid my knee-jerk negative reaction to her "good-bye, virginity!" announcement might be because of my own whacked issues with Scott? "That's really cool. And you look really happy."

"I *am* really happy. And especially happy my parents got home so late, you know? They didn't even suspect. I think they were arguing about something in the car on the way home from Dad's holiday party, so they were totally focused on themselves."

Since we both know her parents have fought like crazy ever since they met, this is no surprise. I mean, they're one of those couples who thrive on conflict and drama.

She shrugs it off as we walk toward our next class—economics—the only one we actually have together this year. "Mat's parents just assumed he was at work, so it was the perfect opportunity. And it felt *right.*"

"I totally understand." Completely unlike the front of Scott's Jetta.

Then I wonder if Mat has said anything to Scott. Probably not, since Mat and Scott run in different crowds—Scott's more an "in" crowd jock; Mat's more the quiet type. Also, Mat's never struck me as a kiss-and-tell person. Unlike Courtney, who's willing to give details—though, in her defense, I'm pretty sure I'm the only one she tells.

Um, unless *she's* let on to Scott that she and Mat did the wild thing. But she wouldn't. No way. Not before she told me.

Either way, I'll be able to tell from Scott's face the second I walk into economics with Courtney, since he's in there too. And if Scott has heard, I wonder what he's thinking about us.

Maybe it won't be such a big deal. Maybe Courtney's right, and it's wussy to keep waiting for just the right moment—like I need a scripted, perfect candlelit romantic setting or something.

"You look serious," Courtney says, jabbing me with her elbow as we walk. "What's up?"

Since this is probably not the moment to tell her what happened last night with Scott, I reach up and finger my new necklace. "If Mat was over late, when did you manage to get this?"

"This morning. I ditched first and second period and went shopping. I wanted you to have it. And besides, I knew this was the day I was destined to wear the skirt. I felt it in my bones." She glances down at her outfit, then back to me, with an *I'm bad but you know you love me* grin. "I changed when I got back here. I wanted Mat to see it."

Midterms are next week! "Wasn't first period your review session in AP lit?"

She waves her hand in the air, totally dismissing me. "It was a special occasion. Besides, I'll be fine. I actually read all the books this semester. Miracle, huh?"

"Definitely."

But she can't skip anymore. Not just because of grades, but because sooner or later she's going to get caught. So I say, "I know you've never bombed a class, even when you've skipped, but geez. You've gotta be careful."

Courtney's grades aren't as good as mine, but they're still pretty decent. Enough to get her into Boston University, which is where she's dying to go 'cause they have a killer communications program. But not if she screws up her midterms. Or gets caught skipping and gets suspended.

I have to wonder, doesn't she care anymore? And is this because of Mat? Or something else?

"I know you worry about me." She puts her hand on my arm to stop me just outside the classroom door. "But seriously, Jenna. I'm not going to blow anything. My life is fabulous right now, and I don't want to ruin that."

Deciding to let it go, I say, "Speaking of which . . . when do I get the details? After we meet the guys at Dunkin' Donuts, maybe? We can head back to my house. I don't think I'll have much homework."

"Sounds good. As long as you tell me what you and Scott did last night." She glances in the door, catches Scott's eye, and he gives us both a once-over—well, he mostly looks at Courtney's skirt—and she whispers, "I swear, Jenna. Yum. You are so lucky."

"You too," I tell her.

Scott slides a large French vanilla across the table, then scoots into the booth beside me, cradling his own drink. "So, you didn't tell me. How was the advanced bio midterm?"

"I think it went okay," I tell him as I open a sugar packet and dump it in my coffee, trying to distract myself from the fact that it's the third time since last Wednesday that Courtney and I have met up with the guys at Dunkin' Donuts, and once again, I doubt the two of us will get any time to chat alone afterward. I *still* don't know the details about her and Mat. And I still haven't told her what's up with Scott. "I had one section I wasn't sure about—"

"Page two?"

"Yep." I love that he has the class the hour right after I do. Not just because it means we can study together, but because we both tend to get hopped up right after exams, so having some of the same classes with the same teachers gives us the chance to go through the blow-by-blow without looking like total loser geeks to our friends, who'd just as soon not discuss an exam ever again after they've finished it.

"I was going to try to send you a text message when I got out," I explain. "You know, to warn you. But by the time Ms. Karpova let us out, it was too late."

He laughs. "Would you believe there was a whole group of people from my class out in the hall looking it up afterward? It really freaked them out. I think most of them missed it."

"You got it, though?"

He nods, like it's a given. Not in an egotistical way, more in the way he would if I asked him if he'd remembered to lock his car before we came inside. Other people would probably find the fact he seems to get everything right nauseating, if they actually paid attention to how well he does in class instead of to his athletic ability. But I actually *like* that he gets stuff right all the time. It makes me feel more secure with him.

He pops the top off his own coffee, then shoots a glance toward Courtney, who's standing next to the counter talking to Mat. Whispering from behind his cup, Scott says, "I'm getting a weird vibe from those two for the last week or so. Something's up."

"Yeah," I whisper back, knowing exactly when that "vibe" started: the night I got my Harvard letter. I hadn't decided when to tell Scott—since apparently neither Courtney nor Mat have clued him in—but now seems as good a time as any. "Things are getting pretty hot and heavy with them."

"That's obvious." He takes a sip of his coffee, then does a double take when he notices the expression on my face. "Wait. Hot and heavy meaning *real* hot and heavy?"

I nod. "I don't know the details or anything, but yeah."

Scott looks as shocked as I felt when Courtney told me. "I didn't think Mateus had it in him." His eyes open a little wider. Quietly, so only I can hear, he adds, "Go, Courtney!"

I bump my knee against his, which makes him smile. Other than the trickle of drivers coming in off the interstate to use the restroom or grab a coffee and doughnut combo before hitting the road again, the place is dead, so I know we can talk about Courtney and Mat without anyone from school overhearing. And even more bizarro, even though Courtney and Mat are right there, Scott and I can go right on talking about them, because they're in their own little world up at the counter.

Again.

"You know I'm kidding about Mat," Scott says. "I know he's totally into Courtney."

"You just weren't expecting them to be sleeping together so fast," I say. "I wasn't either." Or that they'd be so intense.

Scott shifts so he's facing me straight-on in the booth. "Jen, I think they're pretty normal. It's really us who are slow."

"No, we're not. Everyone always *says* they've hooked up, but in reality . . ." But even as I say the words, I can tell from his face that he's not exaggerating. And he'd know better than I do—he's always been the guy on the football team all the other guys brag to about what's going on with their girlfriends. He just has that aura about him. They want to impress him.

But even so, I can't possibly be that clueless. I mean, is *everyone* having sex but me?

I think about some of the other kids in school—those who don't have a significant other, those who are super-Christian, those who are quiet homebodies or loners—and it doesn't seem at all realistic to think they're out doing the nasty.

Or maybe Scott just means we're slow compared with people who are in serious relationships.

"Look, Jen, about last week, when we were at the nursery—"

"I'm sorry about that. I just thought that outside, with the—"

"No, it's okay." He gives Mat and Courtney another quickie glance, but they haven't even looked our way. "I'm not going to push you anymore. You know how I feel about you, and you know how much I want us to stay together after graduation."

"Really?" He hasn't mentioned the sex thing since the day I got my letter, but I wasn't sure if it was because he was mad at me or because he's been busy with midterms and everything.

"Yeah, really. I never want to be without you." He lets go of his coffee cup and puts his arm around me, pulling me almost into his lap in the booth. I tuck my head under his chin and breathe in the smell of coffee mingling with his cologne—a gift I gave him for his birthday back in July.

I close my eyes and put one hand on his leg, loving the way I can feel where the muscles of his thigh meet the bony part of his knee.

"Jen, we have all the time in the world. So no big

rush. We *will* be at Harvard together." He swallows hard on the H word, and now I realize that he's been working really hard not to let it bother him. Or to let it get between the two of us.

"But I'll be honest," he continues. "I think we're ready now. And before senior year is out, we're going to take that final step. I know it."

Chapter

3

I can't meet his eyes after he says this. He sounds absolutely positive that we're going to, the same way he sounds positive he got the answer right in advanced bio. And whenever he sounds that way, things *are* that way.

My stomach does a slow, nervous flip. But I can't tell if I'm just excited about it—after all, my hand's still on his knee and it's feeling pretty comfy there— or whether I'm scared to death. Either way, his complete confidence is freaking me out.

He cups my chin in one hand and leans back,

making sure I'm looking right at him. "Whatcha thinking, Jen?"

Since he hates when I ask him what he's thinking, I find this unsettling. "I'm thinking it's no wonder you aced your exam. You have the ability to see into the future now, huh?"

His mouth hooks up into a smile, but his eyes are 100 percent serious. "Yep. And it's going to be the right thing. We belong together. You just have to mentally relax and trust me. Loosen up enough to see what you really want, what's going to make you feel good, and then go get it. Just like you did with Harvard. I really think that's all there is to it."

He leans forward and kisses me on the temple, then releases my chin before grabbing his coffee again.

Guess that's the end of that conversation.

I straighten in the seat and take a sip of my own coffee as he says, "Speaking of college, before I forget to ask you, I have one essay left on the Brown application. I want to get it out the door before Christmas. Mind reading it over for me?"

"Whenever you want. What's it about?"

"Role models. Someone you admire and what you've learned from them. You're then supposed to extrapolate that into what you expect to learn at Brown."

"Yikes." I look at the warm bagels filling the bins behind Mat and Courtney and debate going to get one, then decide against it. Not so much because I'm watching what I eat, but because I'm not sure I'm hungry enough to interrupt them. They look like they're having a pretty intense conversation.

I stretch my legs under the table so I can prop them up on the opposite seat. "So what'd you say in your essay?"

"I worked backward. Rather than figuring out whom I should use as a role model and then trying to apply it to whatever it is I'm supposed to be learning at Brown, I focused on what I want to learn, then picked a person."

"How to tap a keg in under thirty seconds?" I tease. "You must have picked a Busch. Or one of the Coors."

"Wiseass." He leans back in the booth, raising one leg and then the other onto the opposite bench so his feet are resting beside mine. "Anyway, since I want to major in poli-sci, I decided to pick someone political. At first I thought I should find some famous Brown grad to write about, but that'd be too obvious."

"Too much of a kiss-up?"

"Exactly. So I went with Walter Mondale."

I give him a *come off it* look, then realize that he's for real. "Um, you want me to read an essay on Walter Mondale? I know nothing about the guy, other than he's from Minnesota or Wisconsin or something. He was vice president for Jimmy Carter, right?"

"Doesn't matter," he says, grinning. "All you have to know is that he faced challenges—which is an easy topic to write about—and that he's a role model because he faced those challenges with dignity and grace: all those buzzwords that admissions officers live to read on application essays."

"But why *him*?" I mean, couldn't Scott pick a president, like a normal person would? Or at least some Massachusetts person we actually know something about?

He gets this completely self-satisfied look on his face. "Mondale's son went to Brown."

I should've known. "How'd you find that out?"

"I Googled 'Brown' and 'famous alumni,' and there he was. Plus, I figure Mondale's good because no one else will write about him. My essay will stand out from all those 'ooh, my soccer coach is such a great guy' and 'I've always wanted to be just like my dad' essays everyone else submits."

He wipes a few coffee drips off the table, then two-points the napkin into the garbage can. "So will you look it over? Make sure it reads smoothly?"

"Um, sure." Although, he sounds like he knows what he's doing well enough without any help from me. He also sounds like he's spent a lot of time thinking about Brown.

"Hey, I told you, Harvard's my first choice," he says, clearly having known me long enough to know where my train of thought just went chugging. "But I'd be stupid to just apply to that one school and assume I'm going to get in. I mean, it's *Harvard.* Nobody can call Harvard their safety school. But don't worry, all right?"

"I'm not worried," I lie. "I know you'll get in."
Do I look that desperate to have Scott at college with
me? I must. I certainly feel it.

Which is bass-ackwards, seeing as I'm balking at
having sex with him.

I look over at Courtney and Mat, then back to
Scott, whose cell phone is now beeping at him with
a text message. He's turned away from me and is digging through his jacket, which is lying across his
backpack on the floor beside the booth.

While he scrambles for the phone, I can't help
but stare at his perfect back, complete with extra-
broad shoulders and smooth skin in the space
between his hairline and the top of his shirt collar. If
we weren't in front of the huge windows at Dunkin'
Donuts, I'd lean over and wrap my arms around his
waist right now, spread my palms wide across his abs,
and then kiss that spot on his neck.

And I have to wonder—can you love a guy, really
and truly love a guy, and not want to sleep with him?
Okay—not *not want* to, but to question whether it's
the right thing to do? Even after you've been
together for more than a year?

I swig the end of my coffee in one long gulp. I'm probably just getting paranoid. Scott's not getting into Harvard, my getting jumpy about sex, the fact Courtney and Mat seem not to have the slightest issue with either school or sex, the fact Courtney and I have hardly talked in the last week . . . it's all messing with my brain, and I'm getting nervous about things I normally wouldn't worry about so much.

"Hey, it's my mom," Scott says, sliding his arms into his jacket, then pocketing his cell phone. "I'm supposed to get home so we can go to my aunt and uncle's in Sudbury for dinner. Call me later?"

I nod and kiss him good-bye, and he's out the glass doors before I can even yank my feet off the other bench. Courtney and Mat give him a half-hearted wave through the windows, but his departure doesn't really seem to register with them. And they don't look like they're going to stop their counterside lovefest anytime soon, even if I'm now sitting here all by myself.

I wish Scott could have stayed.

"I've gotta go too," I call out, hoping I sound casual. "I'll catch you later, 'kay Court?"

Courtney has one arm draped around Mat's waist, and her hand is dipping much farther south than it should, given the fact they're standing within five feet of a stack of kiddie cups and a huge cardboard ad for the latest Disney flick. And given that Mat's store manager sometimes cruises by the parking lot just so he can look in the windows and make sure everyone's hard at work. So I'm surprised when she gives me a look like she's shocked I'm going. "Where are you headed?"

"I have student council stuff to do," I lie. Well, it's not really a lie. I have to balance the senior class's checkbook now that all the bills are paid from Winter Ball, then log everything and get it to the senior class sponsor. But I still have a few days to do it, and it's only going to be a ten- or fifteen-minute job, tops. And the only reason I do it at all is because no one else wanted to be class treasurer, and my trig teacher from last year begged me to run—and convinced me by telling me how great it would look on my college applications.

I toss my empty coffee cup into the trash, then pull on my jacket and loop my backpack over my shoulder. Thank goodness I brought my own car instead of catching a ride with Courtney to come over here and meet Scott.

"Are you sure you have to go?" Courtney asks. She looks a little sad, and I wonder if I should wait a few more minutes to see if she wants to hang out at my house with me and talk, like she promised to do last week—though it'll look odd if I stay, at this point, since I already gave them the student council story.

Mat frowns and adds, "Really, we didn't mean to be rude."

"You're not being rude, and yes, I really have to go." I give them a smile that hopefully isn't too fake. I really want them to be happy—I *like* that they're happy—but with everything strange between me and Scott, watching them is just not what I need to be doing.

"I do need to talk to you," Courtney says, pegging me with a look as I push open the door and let in a blast of ice-cold air. "Will you be home tonight?"

"Sure."

But as I turn on the heat in my Toyota and wait for it to warm up, I look back through the glass windows. Mat's laughing and trying to straighten his maroon Dunkin' Donuts polo shirt at the same time Courtney's flicking the back of it, acting like she's going to rip it off right there for anyone who drives by to see.

I realize that it doesn't matter where I go—home, Starbucks, some moon orbiting Jupiter—Courtney's not going to call, and she's definitely not going to come over.

I back out, then drive to the edge of the lot, which is empty except for Mat's car, Courtney's car, and a couple cars that I think must belong to people staying at the Red Roof Inn next door. As I wait for the line of traffic to break so I can pull out and head home, I reach up and finger the necklace Courtney gave me. And I tell myself to be happy she has a reason not to call.

"Hey, I couldn't wait to call," Courtney says, and I'm doing a double take that she's on the line all of five minutes after I've walked in the door, given Mom the requisite update on my day, and tossed my backpack on my bed. "I tried a couple times already, but your answering machine picked up."

"I had to go back to the school, remember?" I actually did go balance the senior class checkbook, since it wasn't like I had anything else to do. But that explains the four hang-ups on my answering machine—all time-stamped within the last hour.

"I wasn't sure if you really had to go, or if you were just trying to be nice. Anyway, I didn't mean to ignore you at Dunkin' Donuts. I thought Scott would hang around longer, and I wanted to talk to you after I talked to Mat."

"I totally understand your need to *talk* to Mat. Don't stress about it." I sit down at my computer, flick the mouse to shut off the screen saver, then double click on the icon for my e-mail program.

"It's not what you think. I mean, yes, I pretty much want to rip his clothes off every second I'm with him, but I actually did need to talk to him tonight. And to you, but apparently we ran you out of there. I'm really sorry 'bout that."

She sounds strange, like something serious is

going on. So ignoring my e-mail (the little flag says I have twelve new messages, hooray!), I say, "First off, I told you, you didn't run me out of there. Second, it's not like I haven't seen you and Mat make out before. I'm cool with it. Third, what's going on?"

"Well, I have some news. Kind of good, kind of bad."

My instant fear is that she got pregnant, but I dismiss that thought even as it comes to me. She'd be way more panicked. But the longer she lets the statement hang, the more worried I get.

Oh, man. She probably got caught ditching class. She had the guy who sits in front of her in her AP lit class turn in her final paper for her this morning because today's class was low-key and completely skippable—a preview of what books we'll be covering after Christmas break.

"Courtney? You still there? What happened?"

"Oh, I'm here. Just trying to figure out how to phrase this for best effect . . . bottom line is that my parents finally decided to get a divorce. Surprise, surprise!"

"Holy—" I have tears in my eyes before I can

even process what she's saying. This isn't even in the realm of what I expected. And even though she's telling me in a jokey way, I know she's completely serious. And she has to be upset. "A divorce? Oh, Courtney, that's awful! When did you find out? How are you doing?"

And how can any part of it be good news?

"They told us officially yesterday, but I kind of knew it was coming." Courtney sounds pretty calm as she explains, "My sister clued me in last week. She said Mom and Dad were arguing about it in their room when they got home from the Christmas party, and she couldn't believe I didn't hear it all. I guess I wasn't paying attention, 'cause that was a couple hours after Mat and I first—well, you remember. Anyway, Anne said that from the conversation she overheard, the divorce has been in the discussion stage for a long time. Apparently, she was right."

I am just floored. "Why didn't you tell me? I can't believe you kept that inside for a whole week—especially with midterms and everything else going on."

She takes a long slurp of her drink, then lets out

a sigh. Well, I think it's a sigh and not a belch, which she's done on the phone before. "I dunno. I guess I thought Anne was imagining things. You know how much my parents nitpick and fight. It's just who they are—I can't remember them ever *not* arguing. But when they launched into the whole talk after we finished dinner last night, well, let's just say I figured out real fast that they're serious. They explained that Dad is going to be moving to an apartment in town. His lease has already started."

I can't believe this. "That's so fast."

"I know." I can feel her frustration through the phone line as she says, "I guess it's in Brookline, so he can take the T in to work. For now it's just a trial separation, but they seem pretty sure that it's going to end up being an official divorce and they wanted us to be clear on that point. The separation is just to be absolutely certain, before they hire lawyers and do all that stuff."

"Courtney, I'm so sorry." I really am. I've known her parents forever. Their getting divorced . . . well, it's kind of like my own parents getting a divorce.

"Thanks, Jen. I'm bummed, but you know, I tell

myself it's for the best. It's weird"—her voice hitches on the word "weird," but she goes on—"and that's the good news in all this. The weird part. They're being so *nice* to each other. Saying 'please' and 'thank you,' and acting like they've been best buds for years. It's like they're both happy about it. I can't even explain it."

I hear her take another long drink, then she says, "Maybe—this is Anne's theory, anyway—they've wanted to get divorced for a long time but were waiting for me and Anne to get out of the house. But now that they've decided to just go ahead and do it, it's not hanging over them anymore. They're both . . . I dunno . . . kind of relieved."

It's whacked, in an understandable sort of way, but I'm guessing it's not making it any easier for Courtney and Anne. "Well, I'm still really sorry. Do you . . . do you need to come over or anything? Get out of the house?"

"Nah." I hear the start-up noise of her computer. "I spilled everything to Mat right after you left Dunkin' Donuts, and I think I got most of it out of my system. At least for today. And, actually, things are pretty cool over here right now—everyone's living in their own little world and keeping their minds on their own business. It's quiet."

"Wow." Courtney's house is never quiet. "Well, just in case you didn't realize it already, I'm here if you need me. And I hope it all works out." Not just for them, but for her.

I mean, if her parents are dealing with a divorce and lawyers, and her dad is paying the mortgage on their monster house in Framingham and the rent on some pricey place in Brookline ('cause Brookline ain't cheap, and no way is Mr. Delahunt going to live low-end), how are they going to pay for Courtney to go to BU next year? And for Anne's tuition the year after that? Even though he's a partner at some big law firm in Boston, I can't imagine Mr. Delahunt makes *that* much money.

"Well, there is another plus to all of this," Courtney says. "At least when I move out next year."

I frown while I rearrange my stapler and paper clip holder. Has it been that bad in her house and I just haven't noticed? "What do you mean?"

"My dad's new place is only a few blocks from the

BU dorms on Commonwealth Ave. Not so close that he can spy on me or anything, but he'll be right there if I need to mooch food or just get away from people. He has a washer and dryer, too, so I won't have to pay to use the one in the dorm."

"I guess that's one upside." Pretty damned pathetic one.

She's quiet for a sec, then says, "I know it sounds awful, but seeing my parents acting all nice is making me think it's going to be the right thing for them. And now that I've had a couple days to absorb it, and I've been able to talk to Mat and to you, I'm actually okay with the whole thing."

I don't know what to say to this. My parents have always been really good together, so I can't imagine being in her place. But I don't see how it can possibly be *okay*.

"Just let me know if I can do anything." I can't resist the e-mail flag waving to me from my computer, so I click on it and scan the e-mails in my in-box. It's most of the usual stuff: spam asking me if I want to increase the size of my portfolio (among other things), my daily horoscope, my soap opera update, and an e-mail from my cool cousin Mark in DC. He just turned twenty and goes to Georgetown, so he's my source for what college is really like.

"You have so many good things going on for you right now, I mean with Harvard and all. I don't want to drag you down."

"Courtney, this has nothing to do with——"

"Okay, okay, Harvard Girl. I know what you can do," she says. "Let's go shopping tomorrow afternoon, before we meet the guys. I talked to Scott about it when I was getting off work at Stop & Shop yesterday, and he thought we should all meet at five for dinner, then catch a movie. So we could go shopping around two? Since it's Saturday, I only have to do setup and then work through noon at the deli counter."

I have zero desire—and zero funds—for shopping, but I click on to my calendar. "You'll be done before me. I'm babysitting for the Eversons from nine thirty to one thirty. How 'bout if I call you as soon as I get home?" Maybe by then she'll have lost interest.

"Perfect!" She starts to say something else, but there's a click on the line as her call-waiting beeps at her. "Oops . . . I think that's Mat. Hold on a sec."

"Nah, go ahead and talk to Mat. I stayed up late studying for advanced bio last night, so I'm going to crash early."

"Okay."

She says good-bye, but only sort of. She's clicking over to Mat before the whole word gets out of her mouth. And even though it's her parents who are getting divorced, somehow I'm the one who feels hollow inside as I hang up the phone.

And I'm getting totally sick of everyone's reaction to the H word.

To: JennaK@sfhs.edu
From: todayshoroscope@onlineastrology4u.com
Subject: Today's Horoscope

Libra (Sept. 23–Oct. 22)
Life feels out of balance today, Libra. Instead of trying to reason out the motives of others, take time to focus on yourself. Unexpected communication from a loved one could give perspective.

Your Leo Partner (July 23–Aug. 22)

Leo can be aggressive and impulsive, but if anyone can bring equilibrium to a Leo, it's you, Libra.

To: JennaK@sfhs.edu
From: SuperMark@emailwizardry.net
Subject: Harvard vs. G'Town

So. Harvard. Early. You've said it now, don't say it again or I'll have to kill you. You know they rejected me not once, but twice. I'm sure my wasted application fees went to a good cause, like paying for the solvent they use when buffing the library floors.

Seriously, though, good for you, Jenna. I am still of the opinion you should come to Georgetown so I can hook you up with some of my (smarter) friends, and because DC is infinitely more fun than Cambridge, Massachusetts. But I'll forgive you if you promise to come here for spring break. Tell your parents you're staying with me (for some reason, they think I'm trustworthy), and that I'm going to take you to the art museums and on a tour of the Supreme Court. They'll let you. Flights from Boston are cheap.

And don't worry about Scott. You shouldn't feel guilty about getting into Harvard ahead of him. Don't take this the wrong way, but I think you'll discover that relationships go through a huge transition between your senior year of high school and your freshman year of college. Not that I'm saying you two will break up after high school—it's more that, even when those relationships from high school do last, they're different. Something to keep in mind.

Let me know about spring break. It's a serious invitation. And I promise you'll have some serious fun.

Mark

Freaky, freaky horoscope yesterday. All morning with the Everson kids and I'm still thinking about it. I'm totally out of balance, and even though I'm not sure about the impulsive part, Scott is definitely being aggressive. (I like that about him most of the time.)

And Mark has to be the "unexpected communication from a loved one." After all, he did try to offer me some perspective on the Scott situation.

Of course, the horoscope didn't say whether the loved one would offer the *correct* perspective, but it doesn't matter. I don't believe in horoscopes. The fine print even says that it's for entertainment purposes only. But still . . .

"Wanna run upstairs to The Body Shop?" Courtney asks as we walk through the first floor of the Natick Mall. "I want to get some of that Nut Body Butter. My skin's totally dry with all the cold weather."

It's crowded, since it's Saturday and Christmas is almost here, and I'm getting to the limit of my patience with people bumping into me with their bags. But it's Courtney's shopping trip, and with everything going on at her house, I figure I'll just roll with whatever she wants today.

"My skin's pretty dry too," I tell her, but since I always get sucked into buying way too much stuff at The Body Shop, I ask her if we can duck into CVS first since it's right in front of us. If I spend my money in here—on stuff I really need—I won't be as tempted when we get upstairs.

Courtney leads the way inside, past a group of teenagers who are hanging out by the huge theft detectors in the doorway, talking about what their plans are for winter break while they suck down their milk shakes from the Friendly's that's opposite the CVS. Of course, they stop talking to eye Courtney for a moment, and I can tell by the little smile that tugs at the corner of her mouth as we hit the magazine aisle that she noticed them noticing her too.

When she bends down to snag a copy of *Teen People* off one of the lower racks, I notice that her jeans are hanging pretty loose. "Courtney, how much weight have you lost? And don't say you haven't lost any. I was with you when you bought those jeans a couple months ago."

She flips past the pictures of some boy band singer and his girlfriend of the moment (because who really cares?) and looks over her shoulder at me. "Not much—I'm not trying or anything. Why? Do you think it's noticeable?"

"Um, yeah!" She's always been a stick, but this is even skinnier than her usual self, and I know she knows it. "Are you doing South Beach again or something?"

"No. But Dad told Mom he wants to take the treadmill with him to his new place, so I've been using it a ton." She shrugs. "I figure he might leave it if he thinks I'm using it. And if he ends up taking it anyway, well, I should probably get in as many workouts as I can before he goes. Christmas is going to be horrid enough with them getting divorced. It'd be worse if I gained a pile of weight from all of Mom's sugar cookies too."

Now that she's saying this, I realize it doesn't look like she's had a cookie in a couple months. She's been doing low-fat or low-carb or low-something-or-other and not telling me, because she hates for anyone—even me—to know she's trying to lose weight. Mostly because everyone—even me—always tells her she's being insane, because she doesn't have to lose weight.

Since she obviously doesn't want to talk about it, I tell her I'm going over to the aisle with the lotion. As I scan the prices, I decide that if I go supercheap here, I might be able to afford something for Scott up at The Body Shop. I grab a bottle of the CVS brand, drop it in my red plastic basket, then walk back over to the aisle where Courtney was reading. She's not there, so I backtrack a couple aisles. I finally see her, crouched down to look at the bottles of nail polish. She's holding one up in the air and looking at the bottom, reading the name of the color.

And at the same time, I see her use her other hand to knock a bottle of the exact same shade into her open purse.

Chapter

4

"Hey, Jen. You surprised me. So, uh, whaddya think of this one?"

Courtney's still holding up the bottle. For a second, I think she must have knocked the other bottle into her purse accidentally, but then I realize I just wish she had. Because her cheeks are slowly turning pink and she's talking awfully fast, like she's nervous about what she's doing and that maybe I saw her.

"I'm not sure," I say, trying to think of a way to call her on the bottle in her purse without either pissing her off or completely embarrassing her. "You don't usually go orangey. Aren't you more of a red or pink kind of person?"

She makes a face. "Usually. It's the blond thing. But maybe I should try this one, just to shake things up. I like it."

"Up to you. How much is it?"

Turns out it's pricier than I would have thought, given that we're shopping in CVS rather than at the makeup counter in Lord & Taylor. Not that I'd be obsessed with the price if she wasn't freaking *stealing* the bottle. Despite the fact I'm cash-poor, I'm not the type to judge others by what they spend, though it's getting difficult with Courtney lately. It's just that I remember hearing once that stealing something over a certain price is considered a felony, instead of a misdemeanor. As in, Courtney can get actual jail time.

I don't think the bottle would constitute a felony, but still. Why is she even risking it?

And why am I not doing anything about it? What's wrong with *me*? I mean, I can't even open my mouth. It's all surreal, because this is so not Courtney. I quickly send a mental prayer up to God, asking him to please, please, let her look down at her purse, see the bottle, and then flip out and say it fell in there accidentally.

She stares at the bottle in her hand a little while longer, then sets it back down and picks up another that's even more orange. She holds it out in front of her, comparing it to the skin tone on the back of her hand, then nods toward my basket. "You buying that lotion?"

"Yeah." You buying that polish?

"Well, if we want enough time to hit The Body Shop, you should get in line. I'll meet you outside."

I say okay and walk to the front of the store like nothing happened. I just don't know what to do. As long as I've known her, she's never so much as taken a sheet of notebook paper from me without asking first, and I've told her over and over to just take whatever she needs. But she still asks. She's that honest.

I glance back toward the nail polishes, but I can't see Courtney. She's moved farther back, in the direction of the Revlon display.

When it's my turn, I hand the guy at the cash

register a five for the lotion, then take the little white and red plastic CVS bag and pocket my change, all the time trying to ignore the horrid sick feeling in my stomach.

I tell myself that this should not be a big deal. But it is. Not so much because of the polish, but because I'm suddenly wondering if the person I thought I knew best in the whole world is really someone I've never known at all.

I turn around to go find Courtney, but she's already standing behind me. "Ready?"

I nod, then gesture that she should lead the way out of the store.

If the theft alarms go off, I want to make sure I'm still standing inside, plastic bag and receipt safely in hand.

She shrugs and starts walking, saying something about the essential oils they sell at The Body Shop and whether they actually do anything, but I'm hardly listening. My eyes are riveted on her funky black purse, which is now latched shut—meaning she either saw the polish and put it back, or else she's really stealing it on purpose. No way could she have closed the purse without noticing the bright orange beacon she knocked in there.

I flinch as she passes the theft alarms. Then . . . nothing.

She's a few steps out into the mall before she realizes I'm not right with her. She rolls her eyes at me. "C'mon, Jenna. I need to go home before the movies so I can change clothes, remember?"

"Right." I hurry past the theft alarms, then join her as she hustles to the escalator. The whole time we're in The Body Shop, I smell the different body butters and essential oils like I'm really interested. I even pretend to read the label on the peppermint foot lotion. But I can't take my eyes off Courtney. I can't help but watch where her hands are at all times, making sure she's not taking another five-fingered discount. Or maybe waiting to see if she does, so I'll have confirmation that I really saw what I thought I saw in the CVS.

She grabs body butters in Nut and Mango, a pack of emery boards, and two lip butters, then walks up to the checkout and plops her credit card onto the counter with them. I try to peek in her purse when she opens it, but because it's wedged between her hip and the green counter at an odd angle, I can't get a good look.

I take a step to the side, so I can get a better view into her purse. She catches my eye, though, and starts talking about how much she likes the body butters as she hands me the bag so she can sign the charge slip. An instant wave of guilt grabs me, and I resolve right then and there to let the matter drop.

I must have been seeing things. Had to have been. One, she's not stupid, so if she wanted to steal stuff, it'd be here instead of at CVS, right? This makeup is more expensive, and there aren't any theft detectors at the doors. And two, she's *Courtney*. And Courtney Delahunt does not steal. Anything. Ever.

As we're walking out, I remember that I meant to buy something small for Scott. I start to say something, but Courtney's already talking about how long it's going to take us to walk back out to the parking garage, so I let it go.

"Cool shirt, Courtney," Scott tells her as we wait in line for our movie tickets in the lobby of the AMC

Framingham. The line is huge, even though we bought our tickets ahead of time using a credit card. The couple in front of us can't figure out the machine to claim their tickets, just like the guy before them couldn't figure it out. Not surprisingly, no one under the age of twenty-one has a problem.

"Thanks," Courtney tells Scott, smiling. I'm glad he said something, too, because I think she needs a little boost after breaking the divorce news to everyone. Of course, since it's the Saturday night of Christmas break, everyone's in a really good mood. We're all done with midterms and papers, but no one's had to leave to do family stuff yet—which means there are lots of parties happening later tonight. Best of all, the snow finally stopped, and it's not completely frigid out, so naturally Courtney wore her favorite T-shirt and jeans and she's eating up the compliments.

As we're waiting in line, I start to develop a new theory about Courtney and her strange behavior lately: the excessive shopping (and shoplifting?), the fact she's losing weight and denying it (well, she always denies it, but this time she's really skinny), and the whole sleeping with Mat and thinking it's no big thing thing. I think it's the divorce.

It's kind of a cliché to say she's acting weird because of her parents' divorce (especially since I'm doing this psychoanalysis on her in a friggin' theater lobby), but the diagnosis seems to fit.

First, she's feeling lousy, so the shopping makes her feel better about herself. Probably ditto for the sex. The weight, I think, is probably partially about ego (and hers needing a boost) and probably partially stress. Even when we were little, she couldn't eat if she was upset.

Maybe—and this thought just now occurs to me—the weight loss is also partially because she's getting naked with Mat, and—not that I'm scoping out my best friend's boyfriend or anything—Mat's freaking hot.

Beyond hot, if you want the truth.

He's got smokin' shoulders and biceps from working on landscaping crews during the summer. And last August, before they got together, Courtney had me do a drive-by at a house in Scott's neighborhood where Mat was planting trees and digging new flower beds. Mat wasn't wearing his shirt, and even from the road I could distinctly see the guy's six-pack. I had to talk Courtney out of doing multiple drive-bys. I seriously thought she was going to drool on my car windows.

I think if I knew a guy built like Mat was going to see me naked, I'd be living on grapefruit and black coffee and doing the treadmill for hours at a time, even if I were running on fumes.

So, having come to these conclusions, I bring them up to Scott when he pulls me off to the side of the line to get us out of the crowd. Well, not the (possible) stealing part, or anything about Mat's abs, but the rest of it.

"I haven't noticed anything different about her," he says, glancing toward Courtney and Mat as they move to the front of the line and Courtney pops her credit card into the machine to claim our tickets. "Well, other than the fact that she and Mat are tighter than ever. But I can tell you from experience that Courtney's bound to be a little depressed about the divorce. You get that way even if you see it coming. Even if you think the divorce is a good thing, like it was in my parents' case." He also suggests that Courtney might be tossing around cash simply because she has more.

"When my dad moved out, all of a sudden he was giving me money left and right," Scott explains. "I think it was guilt—you know, for cheating on my mom and then leaving us to live with Amber. So he and Amber bought me a new bike and video games and stuff, and then on my birthday I got the Jetta. And whenever I visited them on the weekends, at least at first, he gave me envelopes with money and told me to buy myself something I really wanted. When he and Amber got married last year, he handed me another envelope at the wedding."

When I ask Scott if it ever feels like his dad's bribing him for love—which I ask very gently, because I don't want to offend him—he says he never really put that much thought into it. "But if that is why he's doing it," Scott says with a shrug, "then fine. He's not hurting financially, so let him do whatever makes him feel better. Especially if it puts gas in my car and covers my college expenses, y'know? I'm not going to change my opinion of him either way."

As I watch Courtney walk over to us with Mat, then wave off Scott as he starts to fish his wallet out of his back pocket to pay her back for the movie tickets, I think about what Scott said. I can't see Courtney's dad handing her fat envelopes full of cash. But if he is, I have to wonder if Courtney's going to be smart like Scott and put some of it aside for next year.

We walk through the doors into the inner lobby, and after assessing the crowd situation, decide that Scott and I should take our two tickets and head for the theater to grab seats while Courtney and Mat go for popcorn and soda.

"You're right about one thing," Scott says once we're out of earshot. "Courtney's definitely lost weight. You'd think I'd notice since I see her all the time at Stop & Shop, but I guess her deli apron hides it."

He hands our tickets to the ticket taker before we pass under the archway and walk down to theater six. As we scout out four good seats, I say, "So what do you think I should do?"

He drops into an empty seat, leaving me the one

on the aisle, then tosses his coat over two others for Mat and Courtney. "I know she's your best friend, but she might feel weird talking to you. Since you're into Harvard and your life is great, she might not want to get you all bummed out with her problems."

"But that's—"

"I know," he says, and waves off my objections. "But maybe Mat should be the one to talk to her, anyway. No offense to you, but I bet she'll listen to Mat before anyone else. It's just where her focus is these days."

I stick my purse under my seat, then scan the rows in back of us to make sure no one we know is there. I lean over and say quietly, "But I think that's the problem. Well, part of it. She's glomming on to Mat because she needs to feel better about herself."

When he screws up his face at me, I explain, "Nothing against Mat—that's not what I meant. I just worry that she's expecting more out of the relationship than she should because things are bad at home. And having Mat be the one to talk to her . . . well, I'm afraid it'll just make her that much more dependent on him."

"And that's bad?" Scott puts his arm around my shoulders and pulls me closer to him. "You know I don't know Mat as well as I should, but he seems pretty cool. And if Courtney's in love with him, that should be good enough for you. It's enough for Courtney that you love me."

He glances behind us, I assume to see if Courtney and Mat are coming with the popcorn yet, then adds, "You know you can rely on me, don't you? If you have bad things going on at home, or school, or whatever, I want you to feel like you can talk to me. Otherwise, if you can't trust me, what's the point of our being together?"

I give him a little smile. "Hey, I'm coming to you about Courtney, right?"

He gives me a quick kiss, then tells me not to stress too much about the whole thing. "She'll snap out of it eventually. And she *will* talk to you. Besides, for all we know, she's talking to Mat about things right now."

"Okay. I'll try to be patient." Maybe he's right. Courtney's constantly telling me that it amazes her how book-smart and people-dumb I can sometimes be. Even about her.

Scott and I start talking about the movie—the reviews we've seen, the gossip we've heard about the stars—and before long, Mat and Courtney show up with two monster popcorns and a tray with four sodas. Courtney refuses to take money—again—and Scott gives me a quick look to warn me not to read any meaning into it.

As the lights go down, Scott leans in close and whispers, "Just watch the movie. Courtney's a big girl. She'll be fine."

I realize as he starts to whisper that I was actually watching to see if Courtney ate any popcorn. And he was watching me watch Courtney.

What the hell is *wrong* with me? At this rate, Scott's going to think I have bigger problems than Courtney does. Then again, maybe I do. Maybe the fact I don't have something else to focus on during break, like school or college applications or even sports, is making the whole thing with Courtney a much bigger deal in my head than it is in reality.

I give his hand a squeeze for trying to help me override my obsessiveness, and thankfully, when the previews start and Scott lets go of my hand to wrap his arm around my shoulders, I suddenly have no desire whatsoever to watch or worry about Courtney.

"Totally fake special effects," Courtney says between bites of nachos as we sit at a barside table in Bennigan's and plan our strategy for the evening. "But I still think the movie was pretty good."

We all agree. The special effects looked like they were from the eighties, but it was still a cool enough flick to be worth the ticket price.

And, frankly, it gave me enough of a break from living inside my own warped skull to make me feel 100 percent better.

"So what's the party plan?" I ask. I know this cracks Scott up, but now that I don't have college or midterms hanging over my head, I figure tonight's the night to show them I can go out and relax. Also, this way, when school starts up again, they'll be off my case.

Since we went to the early movie, it's only nine thirty and most of the parties we've heard about are just getting started. After we eliminate several possibilities, the guys start to weigh the pros and cons of the two parties that sound promising: one that a bunch of the jocks are having, which Scott says we're all invited to, and one that's at the house of a Brazilian friend of Mat's. I've been to a couple of the jock parties. They're usually okay, but mostly because that's where all the gossip is. Stuff happens at those: couples hook up and break up, or people puke on one another, and it's guaranteed that at least one catfight's gonna start about who back-stabbed whom. In other words, it's where all the beautiful people like Scott do the see-and-be-seen thing, and it's always the party everyone's talking about Monday at school, debating exactly what happened.

There is also, almost always, alcohol involved. Some parents are simply oblivious to the fact there's beer being served in their home right under their noses, some parents are okay with it as long as no one's driving home and no one drinks too much (which Courtney's dad says is a monster lawsuit waiting to happen, no matter how much anyone drinks and whether they drive), and some parties, like the one apparently going on now, happen when the parents are out of town and don't have a clue there's a party at all.

"Rick Dando's party is closer," Scott says as he snags a beef-and-cheese-laden nacho from our side of the pile. "Maybe we can go there first, then if it sucks or it looks like the cops are gonna show up, we can ditch and go over to Lucas Ribiero's."

"If we go to Rick's party first, we won't leave," Mat points out. "It's supposed to be huge, and you know how that goes. Either we won't be able to find one another, or someone will get stuck talking to someone else—"

"You think it'll be big enough that someone will call the cops?" I ask, trying to sound like I'm simply curious and not freaked out. Rick lives in a really nice part of town—one where the neighbors are going to pick up the phone if some drunk teenager decides to take a leak in their backyard. Or hurl there.

"You're such a wuss," Courtney says to me over the chip pile.

"I doubt there'll be cops," Scott says, rolling his eyes at Courtney. "Besides, whenever there are tons of people, you can just fade into the background if the cops come, then quietly leave out the back. They're going to be more focused on trying to figure out who lives in the house and whether they're serving alcohol, or breaking up fights if there are any."

"Meaning, if you have a drink in your hand, get rid of it quick and you'll be fine," says Mat, though I can tell from his expression that he has no intention of having a drink at all. And that he'd just as soon not go to Rick Dando's party.

"What if we do it the other way around, then?" I suggest, though I hate being the one to bring it up because I am clearly the most party etiquette-impaired of the four of us. "We go to Lucas's place, dance for a while, talk to everyone, then head over to Rick's? It's going to be a lot smaller, so we don't have to worry about finding one another to leave."

Really, I'm secretly hoping it won't be an issue, since if we go to Lucas's first, the party at Rick's might be over before we get there—totally wimpy, I know, but I get wigged out by those really loud, crowded parties. And if it's not over, we all have two a.m. curfews, so we'd still have to leave by one thirty, which I hope means we'd spend less total time at Rick's than if we went there first.

I know I'll have more fun at Lucas's party, anyway. I don't think he's a big drinker, so even if there's alcohol—which I doubt—it won't be the focus. It'll be the music. I went to one of his parties sophomore year, and it was the best. I danced and danced and danced.

Scott shrugs. "Sounds good to me. We should get the bill."

While he flags down the waitress and Courtney makes a preventive run to the bathroom—because who knows what condition the bathrooms will be in by the time we get to Lucas's or Rick's?—Mat turns to me. "So, how'd shopping go for you? Get anything cool?"

I polish off a nacho and shake my head. "Nah— just some lotion. Oh, and a pair of tennis shoes from Filene's. My old pair are just beat."

"Courtney showed me the shoes she got. The brown sandals."

"They were on super sale," I tell him. "They'll be awesome this summer."

"She tried 'em on for me," he says, then blushes.

It cracks me up that Mat blushes about things like this, but he does. He has an old-fashioned streak that he tries very hard to hide. "Then she offered to let me paint her toes with the nail polish she bought. I took a pass. I draw the line at toenail painting. Some guys like that but"—he shrugs—"*Alegria de uns, tristeza de outros.* One guy's happiness is another guy's misery."

"She has new polish? I didn't see her buy any." I say this in an offhanded way, but on the inside I think I'm going to be sick.

Especially when Mat's gaze drifts behind me, and I realize that Courtney walked up right when I said that I didn't see her buy any.

"You didn't show Jenna your new nail polish?" Mat asks her as she sits down. He looks over at me again. "It's this rusty orange color. Kind of ugly orange."

"It's not ugly," Courtney says. "And Jenna saw it."

I did?

She gives me a completely accusatory look. "Remember? It was that cheap polish at CVS?"

"Oh. I thought you decided not to get it. I didn't see you in line." And it wasn't cheap.

"I went to the other register. The line you were in was going a lot slower."

That much is true—my line *was* slower than the other one. But when I looked behind me to the other register, to see if I could check out faster if I switched, Courtney wasn't over there.

And it hits me. She really did steal the damned nail polish. And worse, she's sitting there all smug, shoving it in my face and making me look like the bad guy. What is up with that?

"What's wrong, Jenna?" Courtney says. She looks soooo concerned, too. "You're acting really weird."

Me?! Very calmly—because I'm determined to take the high road here, and because she's been my best friend forever—I tell her, "I guess it's just that I didn't see you buy it."

"I think that's when you were looking at that guy over by the magazines. The cute one, remember? So you probably didn't see me behind you."

Scott glances at Courtney, then at me, and for the first time in our long, long friendship, I have the overwhelming urge to smack Courtney. I'm not a violent person, but hell, she's so damned skinny now, I know I could kick her ass. And I really, really want to.

How can someone change so drastically in such a short period of time?

I dig my fingers into my jeans, willing myself to keep it together. Deciding not to have this fight in front of the guys, I smile at her like she's deranged—in a jokey way—about what she saw me looking at in the store, then say, "Courtney, I have no freaking clue what you're talking about." I glance at my watch, then add, "Let's get to the party. Whichever party. Otherwise we're going to miss them both."

Plus, I need time to think about how I'm going to handle this—what I'm going to say when I get Courtney alone. I don't care if Scott thinks that I should let Mat talk to her about her behavior first. This has gone far enough.

Because if it goes any further—whether she's acting this way because of her parents' divorce or because she's stressed out about school or whatever—it's going to be the end of our friendship.

Chapter

5

"What the hell was that all about?"

Scott's been glaring at me ever since we got into his car outside Bennigan's. I don't know if it's because I'm sitting here fuming or if it's because of the crap Courtney spewed in the restaurant about my scoping out some nonexistent hottie at the CVS.

Either way, I can't help getting madder and madder at her and envisioning various ways I can cause her great physical harm.

"You want the truth?" I say once I can get my anger under control enough not to scream out that

I've suddenly discovered my best friend is, in fact, devil spawn.

He lets out a sarcastic snort. "No, just make something up. Damn, Jen, what's got you so pissed?"

"Courtney," I bite out.

We hit a red light, and he looks over at me. "Now you're mad at her for her whacked behavior? I thought you were just worried."

So he didn't catch on. Typical guy. "You know that whole nail polish discussion I had with Mat while you were paying the bill at the restaurant? And how Courtney got back from the bathroom right in the middle?"

"Yeah—"

"Well, she stole that nail polish."

"*Stole* it?" Total shock registers on his face. "*Courtney?* But I thought she said she—"

"She lied." I punch my hand against the armrest. "Flat-out *lied*! I saw her do it. She was looking at one bottle of nail polish, holding it up in the air in her hand and studying it"—I mimic her action for Scott's benefit—"and at the same time, she used her other hand to knock a bottle into her purse.

Boom. A bottle of ugly orange polish, just like Mat described."

Scott lets out a puff of air, then reaches for the dashboard and clicks on the radio. "Wow."

I wait a few seconds, just to see if he's going to say anything else, then say, "That's your only comment? 'Wow'?"

I know I sound like I'm having a major PMS attack, and I know he totally hates dealing with girl drama, but I really need to know his opinion on all this.

He glances at me, then focuses on the traffic light. Very carefully, he says, "Not that I think you're making this up—you know I would never think you would lie about something like this—but are you certain about what you saw? I mean, we both know how Courtney is. I would never think of her as the stealing type, even for kicks and giggles. She's way too honest."

"Dead certain."

The light turns green, and he hits the gas. "So, if you thought she was shoplifting, why didn't you say anything to her at the store? Right when she did it?"

"Because I wasn't sure she did it."

"You just said—"

"I know what I said." I inhale, then explain: "I was coming around the corner into the makeup aisle right when it happened, and you know, I just didn't want to believe it. When she saw me, she put the bottle she was holding back onto the shelf and picked up another one, saying the first one—the one exactly like what she stole—wasn't quite the right color. She was talking fast and acting all nervous, and then she told me I should hurry up and go buy the lotion I had in my basket because we didn't have a lot of time. I was so stunned, I just didn't know what to say. So I went up to the cash register."

"And you're sure she didn't get in another line while you bought the lotion?"

"Nope. She couldn't have. I kept looking behind me to see if she was coming. I would have seen if she was at the other register."

As I say this, I picture myself back in the store and try to think of the details of what happened. "And you know what else? When we left, she didn't have a CVS bag. They always make you take the bag, whether you want it or not."

"True," he says, and I can tell we're both thinking about the time a couple weeks ago when we ran into CVS to grab some batteries and the clerk insisted we take the bag, even though I told him I could put the batteries in my purse.

"Anyway," I say, "when we walked out of the store, I was hoping I was wrong—that she didn't knock it in her purse, and that if she did, it was totally an accident and that she saw it and put it back. So I didn't say anything. But now I know."

He stares straight ahead, focusing on the taillights of Mat's car, which is right in front of ours on Route 9. "So just now, when Mat mentioned her new polish . . . ?"

"She figured out that I know she stole it."

"Unbelievable. Un-freaking-believable. What the hell was she thinking?" He mumbles to himself—I think some of the words are the type that can't be used on the radio without the station facing hefty FCC fines—and I realize he's beyond stunned, just like I was. "She must have flipped when she walked up behind you at Bennigan's, thinking that you were about to rat her out to Mat. Mat would be completely ticked off too—he's Mister Morality. Like, even worse than you."

We ride in total silence for a few minutes, then I turn to Scott. "By the way, you know she lied about that whole 'looking at the cute guy by the magazines' thing, too, right? That never happened—totally made up. I think it was her way of warning me that if I tell anyone, it's going to be my word against hers, and who's going to believe she shoplifted?"

"I wondered what that was about. I suspected she wasn't telling the truth, just from her face, but I couldn't figure out why."

"Now you know."

As I stare at the back of Courtney's head where it's peeking over the passenger-side headrest of Mat's car, I let out a long string of four-letter words, which Scott knows is so not me. Then again, I don't recall ever being so angry or feeling so betrayed.

"She's the one who did something wrong, but I'm the one who looks bad," I tell him. "And it's screwing with our friendship. Plus the fact she was willing to jeopardize my relationship with *you* by hinting that I was flirting with some imaginary guy in the CVS . . . you know, I'm just gonna to have to kill her, and over an ugly-ass bottle of nail polish. It's just *wrong*!"

"Don't kill her. Give her a few days, and she'll realize she's being a bitch." He shoots me a look of sympathy, then reaches over the emergency brake and puts one hand on my knee. "Really, Jen. I bet if you ignore Courtney for the rest of Christmas break, it'll freak her out. She'll start thinking about how she's been treating you, and she'll apologize. She won't risk your friendship over something *she* did wrong. You've been friends too long."

Even as he says it, though, I'm not so sure. "You know I don't mean it about killing her. But she's never done anything like this before."

"Give her a few days, then see. And I hate to say it's not a big deal, but really, Jen, in the grand scheme of life, a bottle of nail polish isn't a big deal."

It's not really about the polish, though. It's the lying. It's the not knowing who Courtney is anymore. Instead of arguing, though, I weave my fingers through his where he has his hand on my knee. "But you believe me?"

"Yeah. You know I do. No comment about you scoping out some fictional drugstore guy is ever going to shake us. Neither will anything else Courtney does or says." When I work up the guts to meet his eyes, I can see that he's completely sincere.

"Thank you," I say. I know I should expect him to believe me, but given how my life's gone lately . . . suffice it to say, I'm relieved to know I can count on him.

I nod toward Mat's car. "So what should I do about Courtney tonight? I have no clue how to handle this at the party."

"Just stick by me. They have their own car, so maybe we can ditch them early and go on to Rick's party. Rick's will be such a zoo, it'll be easy to avoid her there if we—" His fingers tighten around mine. "Wait. I have an idea."

"What?"

He lets go of my hand and picks up his cell phone, grinning the whole time he's dialing.

"Who are you calling?" I ask.

He ignores me as the person on the other end picks up. "Hey, Mat?"

I make a face at him and mouth, "What are you calling them for?"

"Jenna left her gloves at Bennigan's. We're going back for them, but you guys go ahead to Lucas's. We'll catch you there."

He mumbles a couple uh-huhs, then says, "Okay. And if you don't see us at Lucas's for whatever reason, you know, if we get hung up or something, just go on to Rick's and we'll find you there."

When he hangs up, I say, "Since my gloves are right here in my coat pocket, care to let me know the plan?"

"We skip Lucas's and Rick's parties entirely and just head to the nursery. Courtney definitely won't be there, and I bet she doesn't miss us, either. Besides, it's our last chance for time alone before Christmas. Whaddya say? And I promise—no pressure."

I'm not sure the nursery's the right answer, but it definitely beats hanging with Courtney and trying not to throttle her in front of the whole school. Not because I'm in a peace-loving mood, but more because I don't want to be the focus of gossip for the rest of break if I end up ripping her a new one in the middle of a crowded party.

As Scott flips a U-turn on Route 9, heading back toward Bennigan's, I realize that there's no way I can look at Courtney's face tonight. No way.

I lift Scott's hand and kiss his fingertips. "I say you're a genius."

When we pass by Bennigan's, heading for Speen Street and the nursery, I lean across the seat and kiss him on the cheek. And I know I've made the right choice.

At least until a few minutes later, when we're rolling into the nursery parking lot.

"Uh-oh," I say, just after Scott kills the head-lights and turns so we're heading into the area behind the nursery. We both instantly recognize the car parked—lights off—at the far side of the lot, under the ice-laden branches of a tall evergreen. It's a guy Scott knows from basketball, and the guy's with his girlfriend.

Scott does a quick U-turn, trying to make it look like we're nothing more than some random car that happened to wander back there accidentally, then heads back onto Speen Street.

"Now what?" I hate the idea of heading to Rick

Dando's, but there's really nowhere private to go at this point.

"I know you didn't want to go to a hotel before," he says, "and I totally don't want to pressure you, but . . . since we can't go to the nursery . . . maybe?"

I glance sideways at him. He's so incredibly gorgeous, so out of my league . . . and so good to me, it blows me away. "Okay."

"Really? I promise—we don't have to do anything you don't want—"

"Let's just go."

In my grandparents' generation, I know people my age had kids already. They worked regular jobs to pay for food and clothes, as opposed to the catch-as-catch-can babysitting I do so I can put gas in my car and have some cash when I get to college. They were considered adults at seventeen.

But as I walk through the glass doors into the hotel lobby, with Scott walking beside me, I feel like I'm back in first grade and doing something I'm not supposed to. My gut's clenched as if I expect a teacher to put her hand on my shoulder at any second and say, "Jenna Kassarian, what are you doing here? You know this isn't where you're supposed to be."

I shouldn't feel like a kid, I know. I mean, I've always made all the right decisions, because that's just what I do. It's why my whole future's lining up the way I planned. But I still squeeze Scott's hand, just for reassurance.

As Scott tells the desk clerk that he's the one who called a few minutes ago about the availability of a room, and gives the fifty-something guy the name of our economics teacher, I can't help but smile to myself. And when the clerk goes in the back for some paperwork, I whisper, "Um, nice job, Mr. Evans."

"Thanks. I thought it was brilliant."

"No way am I going to a hotel room with Mr. Evans, though," I tell him. He's about to say something, but I interrupt. "Hey, the name on your credit card—"

"I'm paying cash."

"Oh." Now I really feel like a dork. "Um, do you have enough? I think I have enough for part—"

"Don't worry about it. I got Christmas money from Dad yesterday."

When the clerk comes back, Scott signs for the room, pays for it in advance—he tells the clerk he just wants it taken care of—then grabs the key card.

As we follow the signs to room 145, Scott starts to rub my back, just above the waistband of my jeans. "You okay?"

"Yeah." Nervous as hell. I want him so badly—just feeling his hand at the small of my back and thinking of what else that hand might do makes me burn inside—but I'm also starting to wonder if I'm doing the right thing, assuming we actually do the deed tonight. If I'm going to regret it later.

He seems to have it all figured out, and I just . . . don't.

He slides the key into the door at the end of the hall, then steps back, letting me go in first. It's pretty much your standard-issue hotel room. There's one big bed, sporting a burgundy comforter with a paisley pattern (to hide stains?) with white cards propped on the pillows, offering room service breakfast. The carpet looks fairly clean, and so does the bathroom.

"What do you think?"

"It's fine," I tell him as he shuts the door behind us and flips the privacy lock.

"Well, let me make it better than fine." He turns me toward him, tosses the room key in the general direction of the nightstand, then kisses me hard.

And hoo-boy, is it ever *fine.* Within seconds, he has me back against the wall, and both our coats are on the floor near the door as we're kissing each other and holding each other as tight as we can. And all I can think is, *This is it!* The moment I've wondered about forever. And it's going to be with Scott. Tonight.

I think my brain is going into major meltdown.

He gradually slows down, kissing me more gently. His hands come up on either side of my face, and as he presses his body right into mine, he whispers, "You know I love you, Jenna."

I let my hands drop lower, right over the back pockets of his jeans, and just let my emotions take the lead.

I don't want to think anymore. I want to *do.*

Eventually, he eases me toward the bed. It's so much more comfortable lying here than in the Jetta.

We have total privacy and tons of time, even if we won't be able to stay all night.

As he's brushing my hair back with his fingers and kissing my neck, he whispers that I'm going to love this, that I'm going to remember this night forever. That this is the right thing for us. And that I'm the best.

And that does it. My brain re-engages, and I have a sudden moment of panic. He's still kissing me, moving lower, pushing my shirt up and doing wondrous things to my stomach. But I open my eyes, see the white ceiling above me, and think, *Best at what? Best compared to whom?*

All those self-esteem lectures we got in health class start running through my head, making me wonder if I said I'd come here tonight because I needed to feel better about myself after the crap today with Courtney. And that maybe, subconsciously, I thought proving to Scott that I love him more than Bridget or Ashley or anyone else could ever love him is the way to accomplish that.

I mean, have I become the low-self-esteem cliché girl? Is the primary reason I'm here on my back tonight staring at the ceiling because I love Scott and tonight would've been the night no matter what, or because I had a rotten day and I need Scott to make me feel bulletproof again?

Scott kisses me right by my belly button, flattens one hand over my stomach, then looks up at me. "You can't loosen up and enjoy this, can you?"

"I *am* enjoying this," I say as I play with his hair. "But—"

"But." He drops his forehead against my stomach and laughs. "I knew there'd be a 'but.' It's impossible for you to turn your brain off and stop overanalyzing, even for a second, isn't it?"

Without waiting for me to answer, he pulls my shirt back down, then moves up so he's lying beside me, and we're practically nose to nose. I can feel his breath against my face, the heat of his skin. And it's all perfect. Except for this nagging, annoying question in my gut.

"What are you worried about?" His green eyes just radiate intelligence, and it's obvious he cares, even though I know this is absolutely killing him.

It makes me wonder what in hell is wrong with

me. "This is probably a very awkward time to ask this question—"

"Am I still a virgin?"

I stare at him. "Um, yeah. Although I wasn't going to be quite so blunt. I mean, I asked you once before, and you didn't really answer, so—"

"I know. I had a feeling that night at the nursery, when you found out you'd gotten into Harvard, that the whole virginity thing was as much the problem as being in the Jetta." He lets out a long breath, then says, "But no, I'm not a virgin."

"So why haven't you just flat-out told me?"

His closes his eyes for a beat, and when he opens them, I can tell that part of him doesn't want to get into it. He just wants to pick up where we left off. But he says, "I didn't want you to hold it against me. Or think it meant I didn't love you as much. I mean, the first time was a mistake."

"Bridget?"

He nods. "But you're nothing like her, and I love that about you. You're not like anyone else I've ever gone out with."

Yeah, I'm thinking. Bridget is jaw-droppingly

gorgeous. I'm passable. And worse—at least in most guys' minds—I'm a geek.

"Look"—he runs a finger along my cheek, then loops his fingers through my hair—"I love you for a lot of reasons. Not just because you're nothing like her. I think you're smart and ambitious, and when you relax, you have a wicked sense of humor. And I obviously find you beyond hot."

I can't help but smile at him, and I wrap one of my feet around his ankle.

"And I know I can trust you," he says, giving me a soft, quick kiss. "So I want you to trust me, too. I want you to be happy."

"You do make me happy." How could Scott not make any girl happy?

"For what it's worth, she's the only one. I didn't want to make the same mistake twice. I mean, I've had opportunities, but I wanted it to be special. And you"—he drops his hand from my hair, moving it along my back and down to my hip—"you are special. And I've never wanted to be with anyone like I want to be with you."

We start kissing again. And it absolutely kills

me, because he's so unbelievably good. Good like they show in movie clips during the Oscars good. I try to stop thinking—I even let my hands slide into the back of his waistband, to let the feel of his warm skin work like a drug to numb my brain—but I can't. I can't relax. All I can imagine is how many ways this is going to screw up my life and my plans if it doesn't go the way it goes in all those happily-ever-after movies. And no matter how much I love Scott, or how many other people I know are doing the whole sex thing with no problem, I just can't. At least not tonight. My head's not on straight.

"Scott—"

"It's not working, is it?"

"It's not that. Believe I want you . . ."

"But not tonight." I can feel the exasperation he's trying so hard to hold back, and I can't say I blame him.

I let my hand drift up his back, then meet his gaze. I hate telling him no, especially when I can't make him understand why. When even I don't completely understand why. "I'm really sorry, Scott, but maybe I'm just not ready."

"You are," he says. "It's just that you get way too

wound up about things—you know, like school—and I think it's the same with sex. But if you can trust me, nothing bad is going to happen. I promise. You might even feel better." He brushes his fingers against my skin, then grins when I give an involuntary shiver.

"I don't know if it's that simple." I can't make this decision tonight, lying on a hotel bed with his hand inside my shirt. I need to know, deep in my gut, that having sex with him won't screw up my future in some unforeseeable way.

"I hate to ask, but what does Courtney think about all this? Have you talked to her about it? About us sleeping together?"

"Not really." Not in ages. And when we did, it was always a hypothetical. Scott and I have taken things pretty slowly—well, until right before Christmas break—so I didn't really think it'd be a serious issue for at least a few more months.

"Maybe you should talk to her about it, once you two get over everything that happened tonight. See what she thinks—if you're just not able to relax, or if this is something more."

I make a sarcastic face. "Right. You want me to talk to Courtney because she obviously has no problem with sex."

"That's not why. She's your best friend. Maybe she can give you perspective."

"Normally, yes. But not right now."

"No, I definitely don't want you talking to her right now." He wraps his arms around me, then rolls us so I'm on top of him, lying with my nose a few inches from his. "We have this hotel room for the night. Let's stay as long as we can. If we don't go any further than we have before, I can live with that. And if you change your mind, well—"

"Thank you," I whisper.

"We'll get there. If not tonight, then soon. And I know you won't regret it."

"Still no regrets, huh?" Scott says after I stretch toward my nightstand to pick up on the first ring.

"What, not even a hello?"

"I had to ask again. It's what guys do."

It cracks me up that Scott has started our last dozen or so phone conversations with the same line.

I guess he can't help but pressure me, at least a little. But since he bought me a new CD—one I've been dying to get—the morning after we had our hotel room discussion, just so I'd know he wasn't mad at me, and to help me feel better about the whole Courtney thing, I'm not the least bit upset with his teasing.

"So, sports fans. Time for the post-holiday recap." I'm not very good at mimicking an announcer's voice, but I can hear him laughing, anyway. "Tell me all about Sudbury. Was it all excitement and fun? Let's hear the play-by-play."

"Just the usual," Scott says. I can tell from the muffled noises in the background that he's still lying in bed, just like I am. "Lots of gifts. Lots of time listening to my uncle and aunt giving all our distant relatives tours of their McMansion and debating the merits of granite countertops versus marble in their bathroom. Excuse me, their *powder* room. And way, way too many dinner rolls and Christmas cookies and pumpkin pies. I swear, none of my mom's relatives have heard of protein. I shoulda gone to Dad and Amber's. I bet they ate take-out Chinese."

I laugh and snuggle deeper into my comforter. I love talking to Scott when we're both in bed on the weekends, early in the morning. Or on days like today, when it's the day after Christmas and everyone's sleeping off their family-togetherness hangovers. It makes me feel like we're waking up with each other, which is totally romantic in a nonthreatening, non-dear-God-what-did-I-do-last-night? sort of way.

"Everyone's entitled to eat junk once a year," I tell him. "Even you, Mr. Super Jock."

"Halloween. That's my holiday. I'd much rather splurge on a box of Milk Duds than a lousy slice of Christmas fruitcake." I hear him shift in his bed—it sounds like he's got stuff piled all over it, which he probably does, 'cause his room is always a mess—and then he says, "So, did Courtney ever call? You know, with Christmas?"

"Nope. Complete silence since we skipped out on the parties last weekend."

"Wow." He's quiet for a second, then asks me if I bought her a gift.

"Three weeks ago. I even went into Boston and

got it at one of those boutiques on Newbury Street."
I roll over and reach down to the shelf at the bottom
of my nightstand to yank out the bag, then describe
the embroidered fabric belt to him. It's gorgeous—
black with red and blue flowers on it, and definitely
more cool than dainty. It's the type of belt that'll go
with just about anything. "It's so *her.* But now I don't
know. I still have the receipt, so maybe I should
return it?"

"Nah, don't do that. Not yet, anyway. I still think
she'll call and apologize."

"It's been six days since we talked to each other.
We've never gone this long without talking. Even
when we're on family vacations and don't have much
going on, we call at least once to give each other
updates." Let alone the fact that I went to a hotel
with Scott, even if we didn't do it in the end. Big
stuff like that usually gets an instant call from the
cell phone with a "Guess what happened to me
tonight?"

And in the last six days, I've gone from being
mad at her to being sad about the whole thing. But
I don't know how to fix it. I certainly don't think

I should be the one to call and apologize, but not talking to her is leaving me with this totally empty feeling inside.

I hear him roll out of bed, and I can just picture him stumbling to his dresser to find sweats to pull on so he can go down to his basement and lift weights. He's a big morning workout person, even when there's no school.

"Well," he says, "you'll probably talk to her tonight if you're still coming to meet me at work."

He called the Fairway bowling alley in Natick a couple days ago and reserved a lane for us tonight—probably just as much a Christmas gift for him as for me, but since I like bowling, I'm sure not going to gripe. For us to get there on time, though, I agreed to meet him at Stop & Shop.

But since Courtney doesn't usually work on Thursdays, I assumed she wouldn't be there. "Is Courtney working deli?"

"Holiday schedule. She's listed for today, and assuming what's posted is correct, she gets off at the same time I do. Maybe it'd be a good idea to just wave and say hello and see how she reacts. Not to start anything, just to feel her out and show her you're as friendly as always. I mean, this is her problem, not yours."

"No kidding. But if we get into it, it'll make us late for our lane." As much as I miss her, I'm not sure I'm ready to get into it—not in a public place like the Stop & Shop, at least. Plus, after all the family stuff I've done for the last few days, I really want to have some time alone with Scott. Just to hang out and do nothing serious, and to enjoy throwing the bowling ball at the pins and pretend they're bottles of nasty orange polish . . . or the admissions idiots at Harvard who were too stupid to admit Scott early.

"You won't get into it. Not unless she starts it, and I bet she won't. Why make herself look bad? She has to know at this point that you haven't said anything to Mat about her little case of sticky fingers."

"True." I let out a deep breath, then force myself into a sitting position. Another thought occurs to me—he's been to work twice since I last saw Courtney—so I ask, "You haven't talked to her, have you?"

"Not really." He yawns, one of those long, obnoxious yawns where I can just imagine he's got his eyes closed and isn't covering his mouth. "She said hello once, when we were both punching our time cards, but they were paging me to the front, so I just smiled and kept walking. Probably just as well."

"Yeah, I suppose." I'm not sure if I want Scott to talk to Courtney or not. I know he wouldn't bring up the shoplifting unless I asked him to, but still . . . I can't predict anything with Courtney lately.

"Anyway," he continues, "if we do end up having to talk to her tonight, it wouldn't be the worst thing. We might miss out on bowling, but if you manage to work things out with Courtney, I think that'd be worth it. Oh, crap. Just kicked the Brown application all over the floor. Can you hold on a sec?"

"Sure."

I hear him scuffling around with some papers, then I get the sound of his bathroom light turning on—it has a fan that automatically comes on when you turn on the light, so it's really loud. Then the phone hits the bathroom counter (I assume it's the bathroom counter) with a clunk, and I make a face at myself in the mirror above my dresser as the very distinctive sound of liquid hitting liquid comes over the line—with a bathroom-like echo, no less—followed by the flush of a toilet.

Great.

While the water runs (I assume he's actually washing his hands), I go to my desk and start perusing my e-mail. Lots of good stuff, even though there's nothing from Courtney.

Guess I shouldn't hold my breath for a subject line that reads, "Sorry, I've been a total dweeb."

"Anyway," he says as he comes back on the line, as if he hadn't just interrupted me to go pee, "you might not even see Courtney. So don't stress about it."

"Um, Scott? You just took a leak, didn't you?"

"Sorry. It's morning. That's what happens when I wake up. I didn't want to hang up in the middle or you'd think I didn't care about the Courtney thing."

"Next time you might want to leave the phone out in your bedroom. Or just hang up and call back when you're done." Ick. There's such a thing as too much morning togetherness. "Anyway, I'll meet you at six. I'm babysitting for the Messermans this morning, then I'm going to run some errands for my mom. So if you need me, call the cell."

He is appropriately lovey as we say good-bye, but the whole conversation's leaving me with a sick feeling in my gut, and not because of the sound effects.

Even if Courtney's not talking to me, she's going to talk to Scott at work eventually. They yak there all the time in the employee area when they're getting their aprons, and he's constantly harassing her from the cash registers by paging deli for a price check on something.

I can't help but wonder how Courtney's going to act around Scott if they have a real conversation. Or if he'll believe whatever story she might concoct to cover the bull she spread last weekend.

Or if we'll ever be friends again, the way we used to be.

Chapter
6

To: JennaK@sfhs.edu
From: todayshoroscope@onlineastrology4u.com
Subject: Today's Horoscope

Libra (Sept. 23–Oct. 22)
Don't try to predict the day's events, Libra. Roll with schedule changes, even if it's against your nature.

Your Leo Partner (July 23–Aug. 22)
Leo is in a romantic mood, Libra. Be sure to make an extra effort.

To: JennaK@sfhs.edu
From: SuperMark@emailwizardry.net
Subject: RE: Harvard vs. Georgetown

Shouldn't we change this subject line, since we haven't talked about Harvard (or the far superior Georgetown) in days?

Frankly, I think the header should be SEX?!?, but if your parents opened your e-mail for some reason and saw something titled SEX?!? in your in-box, they'd never let you speak to me again.

Why sex, you ask? Because even though you didn't say it straight out, I can tell from what you're NOT saying about Scott in your e-mails lately that we need to have a little discussion on the topic. So you're going to get my advice, like it or not.

If I thought you'd listen, I'd tell you to get a nun's habit and spend the rest of your life with your legs crossed. Tight. But since we both know that's not realistic, well, my only advice—again, not that you asked for it—is to go with your gut. You'll have a good instinct about whether it's right. (Both the right person and the right timing.)

But—while you're thinking about it—here are some things you need to understand, and that your parents and girlfriends simply aren't going to tell you:

1. Just because a guy (not specifically Scott, but ANY guy) tells you he loves you doesn't make it true. Believe me, when he's in high school (or even college—well, make that especially college), a guy just wants to get in your pants. Harsh, but true. Yes, he might love you. But he's going to say it even if he simply likes you a lot. Or even if he simply thinks you're okay. You hear it so often because it's true: Guys think with whichever head is harder at the time.

2. Assume that you will not be with this guy the rest of your life. I hate to say this, because you'll think I'm ripping on Scott, which I am NOT. But relationships end. Even serious ones. Every girl I know who slept with

a guy assuming that he was The One and who wouldn't have slept with him otherwise ended up getting hurt. So go in with your eyes wide open, okay?

3. If you do decide to do it, USE PROTEC-TION!!!! Don't blow this off, Jenna. If you're even CONSIDERING sex you need to get on the Pill. If you're afraid your parents will find out, go to a clinic. You can get a prescription without your mom and dad knowing (and if you even hint to them I told you this, I will deny it; remember that I am the good cousin, the one they trust to steer you along the path of righteousness). Then—and this is important—do NOT tell Scott you're on the Pill.

This might seem deceptive, but it's not (take it from a guy, okay?). If he thinks you're on the Pill, he's not going to be as diligent about wearing a condom every time. And you need BOTH. And I do mean every time. Got it? (If you don't promise me you'll use both, I'm going to fly up there and personally strangle you.)

4. If you decide not to do it, that's perfectly fine. (Preferable, really, but I'm trying to be a realist. . . .) You have to do what's right for you and to hell with what anyone else thinks or what's popular or what Scott wants. Don't take that step just because you think it's what's expected.

I feel really strange about putting all this in an e-mail, so delete it right after you read it, all right? And CALL ME sometime soon. I'm going to be driving back and forth to my parents' place in Maryland this week and next since it's still Christmas break, but for the most part, I'll be here at the Georgetown apartment. We should talk about this. I'm worried about you. I know with Courtney being wacko lately you're not talking to her, but you'd better talk to someone (and no, Scott doesn't count in this case).

All the more reason you should come here for spring break, BTW. You clearly need me to put your head straight, even if you don't think you do.

Ask your parents NOW, before they discover I'm a deviant.

Your older and wiser cousin, Mark

"Hey, Jen!" I turn around to see Courtney's sister standing behind me in line at Bruegger's Bagels, a shy smile on her pale face.

"Hey, Anne, what are you doing here?" I know it's a dorky question to ask, but it just pops out because it feels like the thing to say. Also, I have no clue if she knows Courtney and I haven't talked for the last week.

"Just grabbing lunch." She frowns, then reaches up to touch my hair. "Um, I think you have peanut butter in your hair. You and Scott getting kinky?"

"Oh." I reach up to feel, and it's definitely peanut butter. Anne has already grabbed a napkin, though, and she's nice enough to wipe the strands clean. "I was babysitting for the Messerman kids," I explain. "I made them lunch right before I left. Joey tried to help."

"He's helped me before too. They're pretty cool kids, though, don't you think?"

"Yeah, they actually listen most of the time." I forget that Anne babysits for them sometimes too. "And the Messermans pay really well."

"I hear you there." We move forward in line, and after I order a bagel sandwich and she orders hers, she says, "So I assume you've been talking to Courtney about everything that's going on?"

"A little." I'm careful to not give anything away, just in case.

Anne's eyes get wide. "She did tell you about the divorce, didn't she?"

"Yeah. I'm really sorry, Anne. You know how much I like both your parents."

Anne smiles, but it's a sad smile. "I know. Lemme tell you, Christmas sucked the big one. Dad and Mom were cheery and everything, but since Dad moved out last weekend, it felt really strange having him there. And my parents acting all nicey-nice is just . . . well, you know."

She shrugs as she takes a straw out of the container near the register and peels off the white wrapper. "He invited me to his apartment in Brookline, but I haven't gone yet. Maybe next week. Courtney says it's gorgeous. Just off Beacon Street, in some really luxe building with a doorman and everything."

"Courtney's been there already?"

"Yeah. She spent the day before Christmas there. Guess they walked around downtown and looked at holiday lights and the skaters on the Frog Pond and stuff. She says they talked a little, but she didn't really tell me what about."

The bagel guy hands us both our sandwiches in to-go bags, along with our drinks. Anne grabs a handful of napkins from the dispenser, then passes a few to me. "Dad says I can stay at his place if I want to do stuff in the city on weekends. But it's going to feel wrong for a long time, I think."

I don't even know what to say, so I mumble something about how I can't imagine being in her position, and how I'm here for her if she needs to talk or anything.

"Thanks, Jenna. But I think it'll be okay. It just takes time, you know?" She jerks a thumb toward her car, which is parked next to my beater Toyota out in the parking lot. "I have to go. Running errands and stuff. But I was hoping to talk to you about Courtney, so I'm glad we ran into each other. I was going to call you tonight."

Since Anne's fairly shy—really the opposite of Courtney, personality-wise—and this is about the typical length of our conversations, I'm trying to hide my surprise. "What about Courtney?"

She moves closer to the door, indicating that she'd prefer to talk outside. It's really cold, but I notice there are some other kids from our high school sitting in one of the booths, so she's probably just being discreet. I follow her out the door, and the instant it shuts behind us, she says, "Courtney's really been down about all this, even though she's talking a good game, and acting all excited about visiting Dad and all. I dunno . . . I think she has a lot going on. More than just the divorce. And she won't talk to me about whatever it is. Probably because she thinks I'll tell Mom or something."

"And you want me to check up on her?"

Anne tucks a loose strand of blond hair behind her ear and nods. "You don't need to interrogate her or anything, but I was hoping you could casually find out what's up next time you talk to her. See if this is just the divorce. And if there's anything I can do."

"Sure." If we talk, that is. "I've been worried about her too."

"It might be the college thing, partially," Anne adds. "She's really stressed out about her applications. Especially the BU one. She's desperate to get into their communications program, you know?"

"I know. I'll do what I can, okay?" Which is probably nothing, but I can't bring myself to tell her that.

Anne gives me a quickie hug. "Thanks. You're the best."

But as she slides into her car and I get in mine, I feel like anything but the best. I feel like a fraud of a friend, to both her and Courtney.

I'm going to have to go in.

I use the sleeve of my sweater to swipe the fog from my car window before squinting at the entrance of the Stop & Shop. Unfortunately, I can't see a thing inside the store. There are too many sale posters with pictures of scallops and various canned goods at

LOW, LOWER, LOWEST! prices plastered to the store windows, blocking my view.

Either Scott's waiting inside because he can't see my car where it's parked near the back of the lot or he's been held up. Either way, I'm screwed.

I give the Toyota key a half-turn, just enough to get the radio going and—more importantly—to light up the clock.

Quarter after six.

Courtney should—*should*—be gone by now, since she usually bolts the instant her shift is over. But I haven't seen her come out, so I'm not counting on it.

After taking one last, long sip of my lukewarm coffee, I yank the keys out of the ignition, shoulder my purse, and head toward the sliding doors of the Stop & Shop, careful not to step in any of the puddles filling the parking lot. I loathe having to do this, but if I don't find Scott soon, we'll miss our lane reservation.

And with any luck, Courtney was one of those people I saw walking out hunched under an umbrella and I just couldn't tell.

As soon as the electronic eye swishes the doors

open for me, I realize I'm just the queen of wishful thinking. Courtney's still here, standing about thirty feet away, right next to the row of can and bottle recycling machines. She's talking to Scott—of course—but neither one of them looks happy.

In fact, they look really intense. *Great.* Courtney's probably getting into it with him.

I'm about to call out, "Hey, Scott," thinking that if I act all cheery and like I have no clue they might be in the middle of some serious discussion, then I can get him away from Courtney before things go south. And while we still might get our lane.

But for whatever reason—maybe the look of complete pissedness on Courtney's face as she's talking to Scott—I hesitate, stopping right inside the doors next to the rows of dripping wet shopping carts that some poor person pushed in from the parking lot for minimum wage.

Now what? Do I interrupt? Go right back out the door and pretend I never came inside? No, that won't work. They'd probably see me walking out.

Crap. I suck at knowing what to do in a situation like this.

"Look, I gotta go. Jen must be here by now. But say a word and you're dead meat," I hear Scott tell Courtney. He's not particularly loud. I can barely hear him from the front doors. And he doesn't sound angry at all. He's using that calm, determined voice he has when he's certain he's correct about something.

But Courtney looks like she'd give him a swift kick to his privates if they weren't standing in a public place. "Fine." She crosses her arms over her chest, mushing the Stop & Shop logo on her deli apron. "But you'd better not do it. Or *you're* dead meat. I swear, Scott, I'll tell her. I'll tell everyone. And I don't care what you do to me."

"I told you, I'm not doing it, so just forget I said anything."

He takes a couple steps backward, toward the doors, and I figure I'd better make my presence known or risk getting caught. I start walking forward, but I keep my head down, using one hand to brush the rainwater off my hair, pretending like I haven't seen them yet. When I look up, they're both turned toward me. Scott's got a huge smile on his face, but Courtney looks uncomfortable. Not pissed anymore, but definitely uncomfortable.

Well, if Scott told her that the two of us know that she's been shoplifting, she *should* be uncomfortable. But what in the world could Scott be telling her to keep secret? And what does Courtney not want Scott to do? Talk to me about their conversation, since I'm guessing I'm the subject du jour? The only other "her" I can imagine them discussing is their store manager.

"Hey, guys!" I force myself to be all happy-smiley as I approach. "Store looks dead tonight."

They both shrug, then Scott says, "Sorry I'm running late. I had to restock plastic bags on all the checkout aisles. We're going to have to hurry."

"I think we can make it if we leave right now." I give Courtney a quick look. Just to be friendly— since I'm determined to stick to the high road here— I say, "Catch you later, Courtney. Hope you and Mat are doing something fun tonight."

"Just renting a movie with some of Mat's friends. Mike Braga, Lucas Ribiero, all those guys." She gives me a smile that looks hopeful, like she wants me to ditch my plans and come with her. "I heard Mike is bringing some girl from Ashland, so we're all going to torture her, just to see if she's really good enough for him."

"Sounds like it'll be a blast," I tell her. And I mean it—they're all really cool guys. They don't drink or do anything wild when they get together, but they're all smart and funny and they laugh a lot. Nights with them are low-key and *fun*. But this one time, I'm just as happy to be missing out on one of their get-togethers. Courtney and I need to settle this on our own. No witnesses, no external influence. "Hope you have a good time."

Scott zips his jacket and says good-bye to Courtney, and I feel my insides relax as we turn and head for the exit.

"Hey Jenna, wait up."

So much for dodging that bullet.

"What's up?" I pause, glance at Scott, then turn around and face Courtney, deciding to play dumb. Since I've never come out to her face and told her that I know about the nail polish—in fact, I've essentially covered her ass by not telling Mat straight out that she stole it—what can she possibly say to me? Is she going to be brave enough to say she's sorry for making up that bull about the guy in the CVS?

"I just . . . I missed getting to talk to you before Christmas. I went to Brookline to see my dad, and things have just been crazy with my parents announcing their news to all the relatives." She rolls her eyes. "You wouldn't believe it. It's like every aunt and uncle and cousin wants to take me out to make me feel better or something. So I'm sorry I haven't called or e-mailed or anything."

So. She's gonna play it like that scene in Bennigan's never happened. O-kay. But at least she's sorry she hasn't talked to me. It's a start.

"Don't worry about it, Court," I say. "I figured things were insane, with the holidays and all." I want to tell her I was worried about her, about how she's doing with her parents. But I'm not sure I should. Not until we clear everything else up.

She plays with the strings on her deli apron, then glances at the clock that hangs over the sliding doors before looking back at me. I can tell she's torn between letting us leave so we're not late to the bowling alley—she can't walk out with us, because she clearly hasn't been to her locker to get her coat or punch out yet—and trying to get me to stay and talk.

"Um, I still have your Christmas present," she says. "It's at home, but I'm dying to give it to you."

So she did get me something. I wonder how long ago. "I have a gift for you too—"

"Maybe you guys can get together tomorrow and exchange, when you have more time to talk," Scott interrupts. "I don't mean to be rude, Courtney, but we're going to miss our reservation."

"I'll call you tomorrow." Courtney looks completely sincere as she says it, and even though there's not a hint of apology in her tone, I can see it in her expression.

"Okay." Maybe things aren't going to be as bad as I thought. I can't see how we can be the kind of tight friends we've always been if the whole stealing thing is just left unspoken between us, and I'm hoping Courtney realizes it too. "Call before noon, though. I might be babysitting in the afternoon. I'm trying to take on as many jobs as I can over break."

"Promise."

Scott grabs my hand, and we hurry through the

glass doors. He stops just outside, under the store's overhang, then looks at me. "Which car?"

"Yours. Definitely."

He grins, and we scramble across the parking lot and into the Jetta as fast as we can, getting soaked with every step.

"I hate the rain," he says as he yanks his door shut. "Especially on top of all the snow. It's going to be icy and gross for the next week. You know it's supposed to get cold again tomorrow and snow on top of all this rain?"

I didn't know, but I don't care, either. "Maybe after college we can get jobs in California. Or Florida. Someplace without Massachusetts weather."

He doesn't say anything, probably because he loves Boston and can't even think about living anywhere else. And because he knows I don't really mean it either. So I ask, "What was all that about with Courtney?"

He slides a glance at me as he pulls out of the parking lot and turns eastbound onto Route 9. "What do you mean?"

"When I came in, you were both at the front of

the store. Were you two talking long? I mean, did you say anything to her? You know, about the nail polish?"

"Nah." He fixes a twist in his seat belt as he drives. "You didn't seem to want me to, so I didn't."

"Oh." Then what in the world were they talking about? Why didn't he want her to say anything about whatever it was, on threat of being dead meat? And why was she telling him not to "do" whatever it was? Their whole conversation still doesn't make sense to me, and what I saw was too intense to be about store-related stuff, like if she had to report Scott to their manager for not ringing up provolone at a sale price or something.

"She came up at the end of the shift," Scott says, apparently able to tell from my mood that I need a better explanation. "I think she wanted to talk about you, but I thought it'd be better to not get in the middle of it, so I started talking to her about her college applications and stuff before she could say anything else."

"Is she getting things pulled together?" I know she was planning to work on her essays over break, because she asked me—well, before the mall incident—if I'd help her out.

"I guess. I think she's worried about getting into BU She says she might apply to Syracuse now too. Apparently they have a good communications program there."

Courtney in Syracuse? "She's never mentioned Syracuse to me."

He shrugs as he clicks on his blinker and changes lanes. "Sounded like the whole idea just occurred to her. Or maybe she doesn't want you to know, in case you'll get upset if she goes to a college outside of Boston where you can't see each other as much. Or something like that."

"Maybe that's it." But I don't think so.

"Hey, don't tell her I told you, okay? She probably won't end up applying there, so no need to get into it."

"I wasn't," I say, because my gut is telling me that the Syracuse thing is totally made up, that something else is going on and he doesn't want to spill the beans.

I just have to hope I can trust him. Trust that maybe he *was* talking to Courtney behind my back, hoping to patch things up between us and not wanting me to know he was trying. I could totally see him doing that. And each of them making the other promise not to talk about it.

"Jen, it'll work out. She said she wanted to give you your Christmas gift, and she seemed really anxious to talk to you. Wait and see what comes of it."

I agree, though every time he opens his mouth, I only have more questions. Did he tell Courtney I got her a gift? Did he use that fact to poke Courtney into talking to me again?

And if so, is that going to be a good thing?

I wish I would've gone into the store a couple minutes earlier. Maybe I'd have heard enough of what they were saying to know for certain.

Scott changes the subject to bowling, though, and a flash of excitement lights his eyes when he suggests we place bets on our scores. As he talks, I gradually feel comfortable again. Like we're the same two people we've always been. Competitive, driven, connected.

Like we're viewing the world through the same pair of glasses.

And like my flaking out at the hotel is something he really can live with.

He must be feeling the connection too, because when we're forced to stop and wait for an eighteen-wheeler to move off of Route 9, where it's blocking traffic as it backs into the parking lot of a furniture store, he leans over and kisses me. "I love you, Jen," he whispers. He's looking at me with a smile so decadent, it would make any female want to grab him and hold him forever, and it makes me realize how lucky I am.

He believes in *us,* and in what we have. And he's willing to wait for me—when a lot of guys would've gotten fed up, given the hotel incident—and do what's best for both of us.

Which makes me realize that if he believes things will work out between Courtney and me, then I need to allow myself to believe it too.

"I can't believe we're eating ice cream in the dead of winter," I tell Scott as he hands me a cone. Triple chocolate, of course.

"I can't believe this place is open. I noticed it

yesterday when I had to drive a Christmas gift over here to a friend of my mom's." He takes a few licks of his mint chocolate chip, then winks at me. "I knew you'd love it, though."

The look on his face is pure adoration. Not for the ice cream, but for me.

As he talks about how he even looked at the ice cream flavors to make sure they'd have my faves, I realize that the look on his face—the same look he gave me on the way to the bowling alley, the look that always reminds me of how Scott and I connect on so many levels—is the same look Mat gives Courtney.

My brain seems to pause as I notice our economics teacher, Mr. Evans, walk up to the counter, order a grilled chicken sandwich to go, then stand off to the side to wait. When he gives me a smile and a wave, I suddenly flash to the image of Scott standing at the hotel counter, telling the clerk he wanted a room for Mr. Evans.

"You all right?" Scott asks. When I smile at Mr. Evans, though, Scott just grins at me and says, "Oh. Gotcha. Didn't see him come in."

I watch Scott clean a bright green ice cream drip off the table with his napkin. He folds the dirty napkin, then slides it to catch any more drips that might fall—a habit he picked up from me, the neat freak. And I slowly begin to grasp why Courtney felt secure enough to sleep with Mat. Why she and Mat suddenly seem like they're in a different world from the rest of us, and why she's so incredibly happy with him. How it's not just sex, for either of them.

It's love. A connection that's simply indescribable.

And it also hits me that, while sex might be fine for Courtney and Mat, it's not fine for me. I did the absolute right thing at the hotel when I balked.

I watch as Scott's tongue stops a stream of melting ice cream from traveling down the side of his cone, then I swallow hard.

I want Scott more than ever, but I also know, deep in my gut, that I want to wait. Not because of religious beliefs, really, or because I'm afraid I might get some heinous STD. Not even because of Mark's warnings that Scott might dump me and I'll regret having slept with him—though I do get a flash of fear every single time I see one of the homecoming queen types eye him with more than a slight case of lust.

It's all of those things, in small ways. Most of all, though, it's that I love Scott enough to know how much having sex with him is going to affect me, and right now my primary goal in life is to finish out my senior year and make salutatorian. To have Mr. Evans and all my other teachers still think of me as one of the best students who's ever graduated from South Framingham High School. To have a clear head when I start college at Harvard, so I can do just as well there as I have the past few years. To never, ever have to rely on anyone else to earn a living for me, or pay my bills, or have to cover any of the other things I want to do in life. I want to have complete control.

I've worked too hard to be distracted, and moving our relationship to the next level will more than distract me. Maybe that makes me a prude or a geek, but it's who I am, and it's what keeps me feeling bulletproof. Staying away from distractions. Staying the course. Spending that extra ten minutes to get the calc problem right, even when my friends are just slapping something onto the page to get it turned in on time.

I smile to myself, then take a huge bite of my triple chocolate. This isn't how people are supposed to get those "hit by lightning" realizations. I mean, they're supposed to actually get hit by lightning. Or a truck. Or have some other life-altering episode wake them up to the fact they haven't been living life the way they want to, and so they change. These things don't happen over ice cream at the Ashland Tasty Treat with Mr. Evans standing nearby, waiting for his sandwich.

Guess my horoscope was right. There was no way I could have predicted today's events: from my conversation with Anne, to running into Courtney, to making the most wild—and yet the most basic—realization of my life. That I've worked hard for what I have, and I can't let myself risk that success.

And, of course, there was the other part of the horoscope. Scott's part, about Leo being in a romantic mood.

I have no clue how I'm going to break the news to Scott about the whole sex thing—that I don't *want* to relax, that I like being this uptight, wonky me that I am. I'm going to have to think about the best way to explain it, but as I start to crunch the side of my cone, I know I've never been more sure of anything in my life. Or more at peace with myself.

And I also know that, from now on, no matter whether it's Scott or Courtney or whomever, I'm not going to allow pressure from anyone else to influence my life any more than I can help it. I know myself best, and I'm simply going to do what's best for me.

If they love me, they'll know it's best all around.

Chapter

7

"Jenna, this is incredible! You know how fabulous this belt is gonna look with my new jeans? Or with that pair of black pants Anne gave me for Christmas?"

Courtney's standing in front of the full-length mirror in my room. She's wearing an old pair of Levi's and a figure-hugging, low-cut blue sweater I remember her getting at Daffy's in New York City a couple years ago when her mom took us there shopping for the weekend. She looks mind-blowingly good, despite not even having on any makeup.

"I think it looks pretty fabulous just like that," I say. "I'm glad you like it." It feels awkward that we're being so giggly and girly given the Bennigan's thing, but I'm doing my best to roll with the moment, to not worry about what's going on with her, but to focus on the life I can control: mine.

"It's going to go with everything," Courtney agrees, doing a final spin and finishing it with a little butt wiggle. Not that she has much of a butt to wiggle these days. The belt I bought her is on its tightest hole.

"Should I have gotten a smaller one?" I ask. "I still have the receipt. I can exchange it if you—"

"No way! It's great!" She plunks down onto my bed. "I know I'm looking skinny, but just wait. With all the Christmas cookies still floating around my house and with the treadmill at Dad's place now, I'm gonna start busting out of everything. Even Anne's griping that she feels like a slug, and you know how she is."

"Yeah." Totally mellow about food-exercise-clothes. Those things just aren't on her radar.

"So." Courtney's eyes open wider, and she nods toward the foot of my bed. "Are you gonna open that or what?"

"I still can't believe you got me a gift," I say, since I know she shops at the last possible minute (and sometimes even later—like, the day after Christmas or someone's birthday) and probably hadn't bought anything for me when things went all insane between us.

"Of course I got you a gift."

She sounds totally offended, which makes me uncomfortable, so I cover by saying, "Well, it's just that you bought me that gorgeous necklace right before break. I didn't expect you to get me a Christmas gift on top of it."

"That was a Harvard gift," she says, relaxing back against my headboard. She looks less wary, which I assume means we're cool. "A once-in-a-lifetime kind of thing, you know? It doesn't count for Christmas. So sit. Open."

I sit down on the end of the bed and pick up the red and green gift bag. There's a picture of a Norman Rockwell Santa on the outside and tons of white tissue paper inside. "Should I guess first?"

"Of course! Isn't that the rule?"

We did that with all our gifts when we were in junior high. It was always something like bubble gum-flavored lip gloss or whatever Japanese-comic-of-the-moment we both wanted, so our guesses were pretty accurate. And it feels like old times to guess now, even when we're way past gifts like mini-purses with kitties on them.

"Socks," I say, with an obviously fake grin on my face, then add, "no, no, it's gotta be underwear. White cotton with pink flowers, the kind I've always wanted."

"Ooooh, that'd be very sexy . . . just the kind of thing I'd give you, too."

I push aside the tissue paper, then lift out a neatly folded top that feels incredibly soft. I spread it out on the bed, and I can't help but think, *Whoa*. It's sheer aqua, but with a greenish layer underneath. The whole effect is ethereal. It's the kind of thing a mermaid would wear. "Courtney, this is really, really nice. It feels like silk."

"I think it is." She leans forward and flips the hem up, looking for a tag on the inside seam. "Yep, silk. But hand-washable. I thought the color would look good on you."

"It's perfect." And it really is. It's definitely

something for spring or summer, and I know I'm going to wear it the first day it's warm enough. "You have the best taste. Thank you!"

She leans forward and gives me a quick hug. I've never felt awkward when she hugs me, but I'm surprised that it doesn't feel awkward now, given what's happened the last few weeks. "Anything for my best friend," she says.

When she eases back, she gives me a half-smile. "Look, I'm really sorry I've been such an ass lately."

I want an explanation, but instead of asking for one, I force myself to exercise some common sense and just say, "It's okay."

Why get pissy with her when she obviously wants to patch things up? It probably wouldn't do any good to tell her what I really think, anyway.

"You're the best." She bites her lower lip, and I figure we're done talking about it, until she adds, "And I promise not to skip class anymore. I know it stresses you out, and I'm sorry. I really do appreciate that you worry about me."

"Always," I say, though it's not the apology I was hoping for.

"And I'm also sorry about the whole thing at Bennigan's."

That's the one. "Hey, no big thing."

I suppose it would have been a big thing if she'd made her apology the day after it happened. Or even yesterday. But now I feel different about it. About *myself*. It's the whole lightning bolt moment I had yesterday. It didn't just dissipate when Scott and I left the Ashland Tasty Treat. In fact, it was the first thing I thought of this morning, and it made me feel completely, totally happy. Like I'm back in sync with the world. I even spent the morning surfing the class offerings at Harvard, planning ahead. Geeky, but totally reassuring in an I'm-taking-care-of-myself kind of way.

So if she's going to explain about Bennigan's, it's going to be because she wants to, not because I make her. I'm determined to stick to my resolution to live my life the way I want, with my own goals firmly in mind, and not live in reactionary mode to the screwed-up people around me.

"Well, I feel bad about it," Courtney says. "I was trying to cover my own ass on the nail polish, and it made you look like a liar."

Holy shit! Is she going to confess to stealing the polish? Ever since Christmas, I've been wishing the old Cool Courtney would come back and replace Whacked Courtney.

"Anyway," she continues, "I know you were all worked up about how much money I spent on that skirt, and on your necklace—"

"Not really—"

"Yeah you were." She gives me a look meant to shut me up, and since I promised myself I would let her talk, I wave for her to go ahead. Besides, I want her to come clean so things will be comfortable between us again.

"The thing is," she explains, "Mat's been on my case too. He thinks I'm shopping too much and spending money I really need to be saving for college expenses, especially since my parents are divorcing and all."

"Mat said that?"

She shoots me a little half-smile. "I know I'm making him sound like a nag, but he's so not. He really worries about me, and he wants me to be able to do whatever I want with my life. So he's been telling me—in a very gentle and nonpreachy way—to be careful."

"That's kind of sweet, in a way. He obviously wants what's best for you."

"Yeah, he does." She blushes, then looks down at the bedspread. "And I love that he does. But when I bought that polish, I just knew he'd freak. It was *so* expensive. So I lied and said I bought the bottle at CVS, so he'd think it was, like, five bucks or something. If that makes sense."

"I guess," I say, because it would if she was freaking *telling the truth.* Is she really this deluded? Should I call her on it? Tell her that she's being Whacked Courtney? Or will that ruin our friendship for good? Unable to help myself, I ask, "So, if you didn't buy it at CVS, where'd you get it?"

"Filene's. You were over in shoes, waiting for the woman to bring you your size. I was wandering at the end of the shoe section—remember?—and that's when I saw it, across the aisle at the Chanel counter. It just called to me. I know I shouldn't have, but since I didn't have anything like it, I bought it." She shakes her head and groans. "And then I saw a color almost like it in CVS for less than half the price!"

"The one you showed me." Pukey electric orange.

"Right."

I try not to look angry. I try not to *be* angry. This is her problem. Not mine. *Not mine.* Even if she's been my best friend forever and we've always fit like opposite pieces of the same puzzle.

She adds, "If we weren't in such a hurry, I'd have taken back the Chanel and bought the one at CVS, but I still wanted to hit The Body Shop, and"—she shrugs, but all I can think is, *Shut up, shut up, shut up,* as she keeps talking—"the money doesn't matter now, I s'pose, but I shouldn't have lied about it at Bennigan's. Or I should have at least told you beforehand that Mat has been on my case about spending so much, so you'd know I was just covering my ass. I just . . . I dunno, I guess I freaked when you told Mat you didn't see me buying the polish at CVS. I should've handled it better."

What she *should* do is stop lying through her perfectly white, perfectly straight teeth. And worse, sounding so smooth and believable while she does it right to my face. Who knew Courtney Delahunt could be such a good liar? And I won't even let myself think about her comments at Bennigan's about my scoping out guys.

"Jen?" She gets two little furrows between her eyes. "Are you still mad? I couldn't stand it if you were mad at me."

"Well, I'm definitely mad." I'm not going to lie about it. "But I'll get over it eventually."

"Are you sure? I'm just so sorry."

"Just promise me you won't do it again," I say, trying very hard not to bite out the words. "I know you're stressed out and have a lot going on and all, but—"

"I totally promise. I'm going to be careful with my money from now on too."

I hold up the aqua shirt. I adore it—I really do—but I refuse to contribute to her problem. And if she's stealing things like polish because she's spending so much on gifts . . .

Crap. Maybe she stole the freaking shirt, too.

No. I will not think that way. I have to trust her. Have to not jump to conclusions.

"Hey, no way am I returning that," she says. "For one, it's a gift. Got it? G-I-F-T. And for two, it was a steal. Really. It wasn't nearly as expensive as it looks."

I am not going to think about her choice of words. I'm not, I'm not.

"I won't say another word about your spending money," I say slowly. "But if you're serious about being careful with your money, stay out of the mall. Tell yourself you won't go for two whole months. Or to the Wrentham outlets, or to Shoppers World, or any of those kind of places. You've gotta stay away from the temptation."

"You're right." She tucks a stray piece of curly blond hair behind her ear, then looks me in the eye. "You know, I'm going to try. Two months. But you have to be supportive. Be my conscience." She laughs out loud. "You've always been the best at that."

"Is that a compliment or a slam?"

"Total compliment." Her smile slips a notch. "Seriously, though, Jen. Do other things with me? Keep me busy not shopping?"

"Deal," I tell her. If she wants me to throw her a life preserver, I'm here. As long as she keeps up her end.

She shifts a little closer to me on the bed, and I see her glance at my neck, noticing that I'm wearing the necklace she gave me. "So we're still friends?"

"We're always going to be friends," I say, even though on the inside, I don't feel quite the same about her. When she gives me a hug, I add, "Just take care of yourself, okay? Do the right things for *you*. Talk to me if you're stressed out about things at home. Don't let the snooty girls at school with all their cool clothes get to you and make you think you need to get something new to be part of the 'in' crowd. And don't feel like you have to be someone you're not to please anyone—Mat, or your parents, or even me."

She gets a strange look on her face, like she's wondering what I really think about her and her behavior lately. Like she's wondering how much I really believe of her story. But she simply says, "I promise. I'll do my best."

I can only hope she means it. For her sake, and for mine. Because even if I'm determined to stand on my own two feet from now on, I really want my old friend back. Cool Courtney. The friend who would never lie or steal. The friend who laughs with me and

IMs me and teases me about being a dorky teacher's pet even though she respects me for it. The friend I respect for being able to read other people and know them for what they are when I have no clue.

And I want her to stand on her own two feet too. No matter what's going on with her or Mat or her parents. Or even with me. I want us to be bulletproof together.

To: JennaK@sfhs.edu
From: SuperMark@emailwizardry.net
Subject: Helllloooo, Jennnnnaaaa!?!

You there? You pissed at me? Did I offend you by using grown-up words like "sex" and "condom" in my last e-mail? Next time, I promise I'll put a big R rating in the subject header, just to give you advance warning.

Or is it because I suggested that George-town might be superior to Harvard? (cough GO HOYAS cough cough)

Your apologetic (but not really) cousin,

Mark

To: SuperMark@emailwizardry.net
From: JennaK@sfhs.edu
Subject: RE: Helllloooo, Jennnnnaaaa!?!

Dearest deviant cousin,
I do not hate you, but I must point out that you
are making some pretty big assumptions about
my virginity/nonvirginity, my relationship with
Scott, and the fact that I need advice about all
this. And, um, Helllloooo, Mark?!?! YOU ARE MY
COUSIN. Isn't it a little icky to

I lean back and stare at the computer screen, then
delete the e-mail I'm typing. I don't want Mark to
think of me as a little kid who needs help, but I don't
want him to stop giving me advice either. I don't
think I *need* it, necessarily, but having him e-mail me
with his views on life (and relationships) does make
me feel better about my decisions. He's a great gut-
check.

Not knowing what to type, I go downstairs, grab
a glass of OJ, then talk to Mom for a while. I bring
up the fact that Mark invited me to Georgetown for

spring break. I haven't decided whether I want to go, but I want Mom to know it's something I'm considering. Ten minutes later, I'm back at the computer.

To: SuperMark@emailwizardry.net
From: JennaK@sfhs.edu
Subject: RE: Helllloooo, Jennnnnaaaa!?!

In answer to your questions, my dear, deviant cousin:

    1. I am here.

    2. I am not pissed at you.

    3. You did not offend me.

    4. Talked to Mom about spring break. She is, and I quote, "giving it serious thought." So I'll have to let you know.

    5. About your SEX?!? comments, well, I'll leave you in suspense about my thoughts. :0

    Your dear, nondeviant, HARVARD-BOUND cousin,

    Jenna

P.S. What the hell is a HOYA?!

"Jenna, I owe you big time. Thanks so much for talking to Courtney for me! I bet it was about college, wasn't it?" Anne's on the phone gushing, which she never does. If I wasn't so determined to not let other people's problems become mine, I'd feel pretty damned guilty right now.

But who am I kidding? I *do* feel guilty. Anne's trying to do what's best for Courtney, and therefore letting Anne believe that her older sister's problems are nothing more than college application stress is dishonest of me.

I have a real problem with dishonesty, especially lately.

On the other hand, I can't exactly tell Anne that Courtney shoplifted and is now lying to cover her ass either. Especially if Courtney's determined to do the right thing from now on.

"Did Courtney tell you we talked?" I ask as I bookmark the Web site of summer internships I'd been perusing and quit my browser so I can give Anne my undivided attention.

"Well, I know she was at your house yesterday," Anne says. "She was really psyched to give you your gift."

"It's beautiful." And hopefully not stolen.

"You like it? I helped her pick it out. If they'd had it in my size, I'd have bought one, too, but no such luck. It wouldn't look as good on me, anyway."

My gaze flicks toward my closet door. It's open, so I can easily pick out the sheer aqua fabric. "You helped pick it out? Thanks, Anne."

"Hey, I didn't tell you this, but it was on sale and there were only a couple left. When I saw it, I grabbed Courtney out of the makeup department to show her. She was planning to buy you perfume, but I told her you'd like the top better. She couldn't get to the cash register fast enough once she saw it."

So it wasn't really a steal, thank goodness. I suppose taking a bottle of polish—one time—from CVS doesn't mean she's a serial shoplifter. Though now I'm feeling another wave of guilt for suspecting her. And it pisses me off that I'm feeling guilty about something *she* did.

"When she got home from your place last night, she showed me the belt you got her," Anne continues, "which you should know I plan to borrow next time I go out. Anyway, she just seemed so much happier. Like she's not in a state of permanent PMS anymore."

"Well, that's good news. But I didn't do anything, really." Just suspect her of stealing the gift. Well, and catch her in lie after lie. I pick at a tiny hole in the thigh of my jeans, trying not to think about it.

"You didn't talk to her about college?" Anne asks. "Not at all?"

"Nope."

"That's strange." She's quiet for a sec, then asks, "So did she say what bug's been up her butt the last few weeks?"

I lean back in my desk chair, kicking my feet up on the desk while I fumble for something that sounds reasonable. "I think she's just been stressed with the holidays. You know, your parents separating, getting her essays written, working all those holiday hours at the deli counter with customers flipping out when their cheese trays aren't just so for their holiday parties. It's a lot to deal with."

I can feel Anne's hesitation over the phone line. "I guess. So you think her mood was temporary?"

Better have been. "Well, she does seem to feel

better. And she actually ate the Oreos my mom gave us. You know she quits eating when she's stressed out. Maybe she just needed a day to relax or something." Since I'm dying to change the subject, I ask Anne what her plans are for the day.

"Nothing major," she says. "Mostly hanging out. I asked Courtney if she wanted to go over to Shoppers World with me so I could get some new boots, but she wasn't interested."

Let's hope she's not interested for a long time. "She's probably tired, is all," I tell Anne. "So, you're going to that new discount shoe store, I assume, since it's at Shoppers World?"

"Yeah, thought I'd try there first. Then head to the mall if I can't find anything cheap. I'll probably call a couple friends, see if they want to go."

We talk about other mostly inane stuff for a while, then she asks if I'm doing anything Friday night for New Year's. "Scott called Courtney this morning—I think it was to see if she and Mat are going out to any of the parties."

"Yeah, I guess this weekend's our last chance before school starts up again," I say, though I have to wonder, why is Scott calling Courtney about parties? Why isn't he calling me? "How 'bout you? Going to any?"

"I'm thinking about going to my dad's. Maybe go to First Night stuff in the city. We'll see. But I did hear Courtney tell Scott she'd get back to him. Sounded like she really didn't want to go to whichever party Scott wanted to, but when Scott said the two of you were going, Courtney said there was no way you guys could go without her. I bet you have a blast."

Since Scott hasn't mentioned any parties to me—well, other than the fact there are a bunch taking place and that he wants our New Year's to be special—this is all news to me.

Could that be what he and Courtney were arguing about at the store? Strange, since Courtney and I weren't really talking at that point. No, I decide, it can't be. It wouldn't make sense, given what I overheard about Scott maybe doing something and Courtney telling him not to.

Which reminds me that I never did get around to finding out about the whole Syracuse thing, which I'd meant to do.

I wish Anne good luck with her dad—since he really is a nice guy, and I want things to be good between them—then let her go before hopping back on e-mail. I see my horoscope in my in-box, but I've gotta get an e-mail out to Courtney while I'm thinking about it. And before I think about it too much.

Chapter

8

To: CourtD@sfhs.edu
From: JennaK@sfhs.edu
Subject: Forgot . . .

Hey—totally spaced asking you yesterday—how goes it on the college applications? Did you finalize where you're applying to yet? I know BU for sure, but anywhere else? Let me know what I can do to help. (BTW—I just finished reading over Scott's essays for Brown. Can you believe he wrote about Walter Mondale?)

Also—thanks again for the new top. You know I'm dying to wear it.

Have a blast at work today. I just know you're loving life amongst the cheese and deli meats. Let me know the plan for tomorrow night and about the college stuff.

J.

Not the world's most eloquent e-mail, but it'll do. I surf the Web for a while, killing time before I have to go babysit for the Messermans again by looking at more internship stuff online and printing applications for a few positions that look interesting. I know I should give a more detailed answer to Mark's e-mail than my "leave you in suspense" cop-out, but I haven't figured out what to say yet.

I mean, do I admit that Scott has been pressuring me for sex? Or do I tell Mark he's way wrong? And I still haven't decided what I want to do about spring break, assuming Mom and Dad say I can go to Mark's. Georgetown would definitely be fun, but the senior class trip to Disney World is that week, and already approved by Mom and Dad. I'm not that keen on going to mouse world, even though everyone assures me that it's a total blast, but I kind of feel like I should go. Just because I'm on student council and everything.

I take a long sip of my OJ, then wipe my mouth on the sleeve of my flannel jammies. Maybe I should just stay home. Use the vacation week to spend some time with Mom and Dad and clear my brain.

I reread Mark's SEX?!?! e-mail, trying to come up with a real response, then decide I just can't answer today. I'm about to sign off when I get pinged. Courtney's online, and of course she IMs me right away.

CourtD: Yo, Jen! You there? I'm reading your e-mail now.
JennaK: I'm here . . .
Court D: Yes to help on applications. I'm sending out to BU, of course. And to Simmons, since I think their internship program for communications majors looks really good. I'm pretty sure I'll end up applying to Mount Ida to make Mom

happy, but it's my third choice right now.

JennaK: Mount Ida?

CourtD: It's in Newton, which is why it's third.

JennaK: Again . . . Mount Ida? What brought that on?

CourtD: Mom graduated from there and loved it. They have a communications program, so . . .

JennaK: Sorry, forgot about your mom. I think I remember you telling me that once. So is that it? Those three? Nothing outside of Boston?

CourtD: What, like I WANT to do more applications?

I stare at the text on the screen. Now that things are good between us—well, at least as far as Courtney knows—there's no reason to hide it if she's applying to Syracuse.

So why would she tell Scott that?

Or did Scott make it up, just like I suspected, trying to cover for something else? Like trying to patch things up between me and Courtney? Hmmm . . .

I'm about to type something jokey to Courtney when more text from her pops up onscreen.

CourtD: Three is definitely it. Unless I don't get in anywhere (but I will NOT think that way . . .).

JennaK: You'll be fine. Like I said, I'm happy to do what I can to help too.

CourtD: Good, because I'll need it! Just don't make me write about Walter Mondale (who IS he, anyway?! I know I should know . . .)

CourtD: And on the New Year's party issue—I haven't heard the final word about what's going on. Info, please?

JennaK: Mondale is a former vice president and was a senator from Minnesota. On parties—I have no clue what's going on. (Although I can tell you that Mondale belongs to the Democratic Party . . . LOL!)

CourtD: I'm calling you now to discuss parties. And NOT political parties. TTY in a minute . . .

CourtD: And P.S. I'm going to pretend you never made that joke. You are such a geek.

My phone rings at the same time Courtney's last line of text appears on my computer screen.

"So, is there a party plan?" I ask, without even bothering to say hello.

"Scott hasn't talked it over with you yet?"

"I don't think so." It all still feels strange to me, talking about which parties I want to attend like it's no big thing, when out of habit I nearly always say, "Sounds fun, but I have calc homework" or "There's a paper I need to finish" the second the word "party" enters a conversation. I keep having to remind myself that, for one, it's break, so there's no homework I'm supposed to be doing, and second, I'm *in,* so I don't need to be researching schools or doing SAT practice exams during every second of my spare time. And that it won't kill my chances of getting into Harvard if I have fun.

But the scary part—the part I can't admit to anyone—is that I actually miss having school stuff to do. It isn't that math thrills me or anything, but having an assignment or two due gives me a goal to work toward, and I'm a pretty goal-oriented person.

"I take it Scott said something to you?" I ask, knowing from Anne that he has, but wanting to hear Courtney tell me herself.

"Indeed he did." She lets out a low Coke belch,

then says, "He wants to go to the party at Aric Jensen's."

"Then no."

"No go, or no he hasn't talked to you?"

"Hasn't talked to me," I tell her. I'd have remembered if he'd mentioned going to Aric's party, because it's not the kind of party I'd want to attend, even if I was dying to go out. Aric's parents fall into the strict "You can't have booze in our house" camp because they're Mormon. They're always telling other parents that's their philosophy because they want other parents to know that their kids are "safe" while visiting their home.

However, the Jensens frequently spend weekends at their house on the Cape and let Aric stay home by himself. Totally misplaced trust, since Aric usually drops his Mormon values the second his parents' Taurus leaves the driveway. He makes a few phone calls, and within hours the house is packed, alcohol flows like crazy, the whole deal.

I'm guessing he hires a cleaning service or something to help him hide the evidence, because from what I've heard about parties at Aric's, the cleanup's gotta be a bitch. And he's never once gotten caught.

"So," Courtney says, "you have no idea if you're going?"

"Well, if Scott told you that we are, then we probably are. Since I was the one who wanted to go bowling, like, forever, I told him he could choose what we do on New Year's." Though I think I'd rather go to one of the other parties, something more low-key. As in, where the focus is on seeing my friends and catching up on gossip instead of seeing who's the most accurate at tossing a Ping-Pong ball into a glass of beer.

"Don't razz me too much, but to be honest, I'm kind of burned out on the whole party scene right now," Courtney says, sounding completely sincere even though she's laughing. "Maybe the four of us can just go to a movie or something? Or if Scott's totally determined to go to Aric's, maybe he won't mind just going with the guys, and the two of us can go to the movies. Or we can ask Anne to go or whoever else from school and make it a girls' night out if you want. I don't think we've done that since Mat and I hooked up."

Courtney saying no to a party? And at *Aric Jensen's*? I can't help but laugh right along with her. "This from the person who called me a wuss at Bennigan's when I didn't want to go to Rick Dando's party?"

She doesn't say anything right away, even though I was teasing, and I suddenly realize that she probably doesn't want to be reminded about the night at Bennigan's. I guess neither of us want to get into that.

"Well, I'm going out with Scott tonight," I tell her. "Nothing major, just running errands after he's done at Stop & Shop, but I'll ask him what he thinks. I mean, a movie sounds good to me, whether it's with or without the guys."

"Great." I hear her fingers tapping on her computer keyboard as she says, "I'll check Moviefone and see what's playing tomorrow, just in case. And I'll tell Mat that it might be movies, might be Aric Jensen's. But let's try to do the movies, okay?"

"Okay." My computer alarm starts beeping, so I tell her I have to go—I've gotta be at the Messermans' in twenty minutes—but that I'll call her the minute Scott and I talk. When I hang up, though, I realize that I forgot to read my horoscope. I click on it, then grab my shoes so I can lace 'em up while I read.

To: JennaK@sfhs.edu
From: todayshoroscope@onlineastrology4u.com
Subject: Today's Horoscope

Libra (Sept. 23–Oct. 22)
A chance encounter will change your entire day—and perhaps the entire week ahead. Weigh your options carefully before making firm decisions, Libra.

Your Leo Partner (July 23–Aug. 22)
Leo's feeling testy today. Get to the root of it—this isn't the time to stand back and simply let your Leo roar.

As I finish up dinner and talk with Mom and Dad about where Scott and I are going to be tonight (they simply *must* know that we're planning on Target, then maybe Starbucks for a quick coffee on the way home, and of course they tell me for the umpteenth time that I need to have my cell phone on me every second, so they can find me), all I can think about is the chance encounter I'm supposed to have that'll change my entire day.

Since it's already after six, I'm thinking my horoscope is wrong. Not that it's ever *right*. I mean, sometimes I can mentally twist it into being right, but that's just my twisting it. But today it's just flat-out wrong. Which sucks, because the whole time I was driving home from the Messermans', I was half-waiting to have a chance encounter.

I even let myself daydream that maybe I'd be putting gas in my car, and I'd bump into some gorgissimo actor who just happens to be driving through Framingham, Massachusetts. Or maybe I'd find out I was the millionth person through the door at the Apple Store and I'd get a free laptop or something. But none of the daydreams felt at all possible to me. I think because the only chance encounters I want changing my life are so totally unrealistic that I can't even daydream about them convincingly.

The encounters that are more likely to happen are the kind that aren't good. Like someone from the IRS seeing me leave the Messermans' and realizing that I wasn't paying the proper income tax on my baby-sitting money.

I drop my plate into the dishwasher a little too hard, and Mom turns around from the table to shoot me a death look—since she got the dishes cheap from some yard sale but claims they were a "real find" and I should be careful with them—but when she sees me cringe, two vertical lines of concern appear between her eyes. "You okay, honey?"

"Fine," I tell her. "Just tired from all day at the Messermans', I guess. Sorry 'bout slamming the plate in there."

She seems to accept this, since she just takes a deep breath and tells me to go ahead and get ready. She and Dad have always kept pretty good tabs on me—making me call to check in regularly when I'm out, always asking me how I'm feeling and if I need help with homework, all that stuff. But now that I'm done with midterms and Harvard's on the horizon, it's like they're trying to bite their tongues and let me go. Treat me like adults treat other adults instead of the way parents treat their kids.

Which, in a totally backward kind of way, actually makes me wonder if I'd have just as much fun staying at home tonight and hanging out with my parents watching game shows or the latest made-for-television movie as I will at Target with Scott.

Then it hits me: What if my chance encounter is supposed to happen at Target?

Not that I believe in horoscopes, especially the generic, mass e-mailed ones. I mean, is every single Libra in the world going to have a chance encounter today that will change his or her whole day and possibly week?

Right.

But as I'm walking up and down the aisles with Scott, helping him pick out a new cordless phone for his bedroom, then walking through the music section to look at CDs, I can't help but keep my eyes open for my chance encounter. Not because I really think it'll happen, but mostly because I want to keep my brain occupied with something other than the thought that Scott might want to head to the nursery later.

He tosses two CDs into the red Target carry basket I have looped over my arm, and we head toward the checkout. As if he can read my mind, he asks if I want to hit Starbucks for a quick coffee, or maybe head somewhere else for, in his words, "a different kind of quickie—not that it'll be quick." And, of course, he assures me that he won't pressure me.

I act all smiley and flirty, but tell him I want to go to Starbucks first, if that's all right, because I'm just dying for a latte.

I have *got* to figure out how to deal with this. He has to know how I feel about him—that I'm giddy in love with him—but he also has to not expect sex. At least not in the near future, even if I have always told him that I don't have any issues—moral or otherwise—with people having sex before they're married.

Because now I realize that I do, at least for me.

I glance at him as he puts the CDs, some Right Guard deodorant, a tube of Aquafresh, and the box containing the new cordless phone on the belt. Will he dump me over this? Will he see months or years of a no-sex relationship stretching out before him and think, *She's going to be in school for a long time . . . no way in hell am I waiting for this girl to decide I'm her priority?*

I take a deep breath and hold it for a second. I need to handle this just the right way so that he isn't caught off-guard. I need him to understand where I'm coming from, and maybe even see that if it's the best thing for me, then it's probably the best thing for both of us.

But if I can't come up with a good way to phrase all of that by the time we leave Starbucks . . . then what?

The girl working the register—a totally gorgeous girl whose name tag reads (get this) Lyric—smiles at Scott as she sticks the receipt into the bag. It's *that* kind of smile. The *if you ever ditch your girlfriend, I'm available* smile that's more than just friendly customer service.

Does he even notice? He must, because he's giving her a *who me?* look that's just enough to make her feel good, but not enough to piss me off if I'm watching—which I am. And it occurs to me that he must get smiles like this from every cute girl who walks through his line at Stop & Shop and every barista at every coffee shop he frequents.

I am so screwed. Or not screwed, as the case may be. Lyric and all the girls like her are the ones looking to get screwed.

He grabs the bag with his stuff. I see the outline of the Right Guard and the toothpaste through the side and get the bright idea that if I can't come up with something to tell him tonight, I'll just pretend I'm on my period. I'm irregular, so he'll believe me. And even though I hate being dishonest, it'll buy me some time.

Maybe I'll e-mail Mark and confess that I'm totally stumped on how to handle this. After he mocks me, he might actually have something useful to say.

When we get outside, I suddenly wonder if Lyric is the chance encounter that might change my day. The one related to whatever options I'm supposed to weigh carefully. Or if my trying to maneuver my way out of a trip to the nursery will make my Leo partner (namely, Scott) testy, since he's clearly not testy now.

"I hate to ask this, but what in the world is going through your head right now?" Scott asks as he punches a button on his key chain to pop the doors to the Jetta.

I look over the top of the car at him, then climb inside and get situated in the passenger seat before saying, "Nothing really. Thinking about my horoscope and all the other random e-mails I have to deal with, stuff like that."

He lets out a little snort. "You're on one of those e-mail lists for horoscopes?"

"Yeah."

This time, he laughs. "You actually believe in those things? You know they're written by minimum-wage, college-age scrubs who're trying to make an extra few bucks between classes, right?"

"I never said I believe in them." I mean, if there were any truth to them, presidents would consult them before making decisions. Astronauts would double-check them before strapping on their gear. "But they're fun to read."

"Oh, man," Scott says, then reaches for his pocket. He stuck his cell phone in there while we were in the store, but now that he's pulled it free, I can hear the low hum of it vibrating. He glances at the screen. "Text message. It's my mom."

"What's up?"

"She's asking where I am. Here," he hands it to me. "Can you type back that I'm about to walk into Starbucks? Then we'll see what she says."

It always takes me a minute to figure out how to text message—I know, totally lame, but I'm more of a caller and e-mailer than a text messager—so by the time I get the message typed in and sent, we're already parking outside Starbucks.

We get in line, and just as we get to the front and order, his mom messages him back. He rolls his eyes as he reads it. "Now I remember why I had it in my head that I couldn't stay out late tonight," he says. "It's money night at the Bannister house."

Money night?

Before I can ask, he explains: "My mom has decided that I need to spend an evening learning how to properly use a credit card, write checks, manage a bank account, all that stuff."

"Um, you don't know how to do that already?" We even covered it in a special class at school.

"Of course I do." He pays for our lattes, then shoves his wallet in his pocket as we walk to the pick-up area while the barista works on our lattes. "She just wants to watch me do it with her own two eyes, I guess. She sees all those newspaper articles and *60 Minutes* shows on how college kids graduate with tons of debt, and . . . well, you know how it goes. Plus, I think she's still freaked out about my dad and Amber buying me the Jetta. She's afraid I think money grows on trees."

"Should we just grab the coffees to go?" Maybe I won't have to use the period excuse after all.

"I'm sorry," he says. "I know we just got here, but—"

"You're leaving?" I recognize Mat's accent even before I turn around to say hello. He gives Scott a halfhearted high five, then says, "I was just about to invite you guys over."

I glance past Mat and see his laptop set up just behind where he's standing, at a nearby table for four. It doesn't look like Courtney's with him, since there's only one coffee on the table and no purse or anything on any of the other chairs. But it might be nice to just sit and drink coffee. If Scott can stay that long.

"Thanks, but I can't," Scott says. "I'm being summoned by my mother. She's got it into her head that I need some parenting. But Jenna might want to."

I'm about to point out that I don't have a car, and that it's okay, I'm happy to ride home with Scott so we can have an extra ten minutes together, but then I remember that I'm supposed to be doing what I want for *me,* not what I want for anyone else. And since I really do want to stay, I figure this is as easy a time as any to start. "If you wouldn't mind giving me a ride home?" I ask Mat, then look at Scott. "I've been with the Messerman kids all day. I need to chill out for a while with my latte."

"I don't mind," Mat says.

"No problem," Scott says. But he looks surprised. Not angry or disappointed, just surprised. If he really wanted me to go with him, he'd have said so, wouldn't he?

But as Scott grabs his cup from the barista and

palms his car keys, and I grab a stir stick and a napkin to carry to the table, it all feels off to me. Scott gives me a very polite kiss on the cheek, tells me he'll call later, then takes off.

As I sit down with Mat, I realize that the two of us have never had a conversation—not without Courtney there—and it's a whole different kind of strange than the feeling I have watching Scott through the windows as he hops into his Jetta, guns it into reverse, then drives away.

"I'm glad I ran into you," Mat says. He shifts in his chair, clicks a couple things on his computer, then shuts it down.

"Whatcha working on?" I take a tentative sip of my latte. Man, but they make them steaming hot here.

"Same thing everyone else is working on over break. College essays." Then he smiles at me as he packs his laptop into its case. "Well, except you. I'm still completely psyched that you got into Harvard. And Early Action, too."

He looks so thrilled for me, I wonder for a second if he's flirting.

"Anyway, I'm glad Scott's not here." He takes a quick sip of his coffee and then, looking at me over the rim, he adds, "I've been trying to find a way to talk to you alone for a while now."

Chapter

9

Me? Alone?

Oh, please, *please,* God, do not let Mat be flirting with me. Courtney's told me a zillion times what a flirt he is, though she always adds a disclaimer about how she thinks it's probably just a Brazilian thing. But I can tell that deep down inside, she's not sure. And she can't work up the guts to just come out and ask any of our Brazilian girlfriends if the flirting is an innocent cultural thing, because she's afraid they'll think she's prejudiced or ignorant or both.

So she just stresses herself out about it while telling herself there's no reason to stress out.

But either way—innocent or not—Mat flirting with me is the absolute last thing I need, especially when I just might be getting things on track with Courtney again.

If she quits stealing and starts acting like herself again.

"What's up?" I ask, making an effort to look and sound as laid-back possible. Especially since the whole point of staying was to be able to have a few minutes where I can be laid-back and enjoy a coffee without complication.

For a split second he gets this expression on his face like he's decided he made a mistake to tell me he needed to talk privately, and he's going to play it off by making a joke or something. But then it disappears, and he gets completely serious again. "Well, this is kind of awkward, 'cause I know you're Courtney's best friend and all. And the two of us"— he gestures to himself, then to me—"haven't spent much, well, I guess any, time alone, you know? Either Courtney or Scott or a whole group of people are around. So I'm taking kind of a risk with this conversation. And I'm not even sure this is something I'm right about, just a guess on my part—"

"In other words, it's about Courtney?" I get the feeling this preamble is going to go on forever, and I'm dying for him to get to the point since he apparently has one.

"*Sim.* Yes." His cheeks get red, right in the apples. "I just . . . well, I think there's something going on with her, and I'm worried. And I've wanted to talk to you about it."

"Something you couldn't bring up in front of Scott?" Does Mat suspect she stole the nail polish? Has he seen her taking five-fingered discounts on other items?

Or is he simply noticing the same thing Anne has: that Courtney's been in her skinny-stressed-out mode lately?

"I think Scott might be the problem."

"You're kidding me, right?" Okay, that didn't come out the way I wanted, but Scott was so not the answer I'd expected. In a somewhat calmer voice, I say, "How is Scott a problem?"

He sucks in a deep lungful of air, then exhales while I try my best not to look disturbed by this little tidbit. "Well, maybe not *the* problem, but part of the problem," he says. "Which is why I wasn't sure how to bring it up to you. Um, did you know they went out together after work last week?"

Um, *no.*

I just shrug, though, and try to look as casual as possible while I tell myself to not jump to conclusions. Maybe it was Scott trying to make things right between me and Courtney. Or maybe it has something to do with the conversation they were having at Stop & Shop involving making dead meat out of each other (though it occurs to me now . . . isn't meat, by definition, always dead? I mean, does anyone say "live meat"? Isn't live meat just called a cow or a deer or whatever animal?).

"Scott and Courtney have known each other since, I dunno, like, fourth or fifth grade," I tell him, even though I know I'm really trying to rationalize it to myself. And to get the image of dead meat out of my brain. "They go out together sometimes—I don't think that means there's something going on, necessarily. I mean, I'm sitting here with you, you know? And we're not doing anything questionable."

"I don't think anything is going on between them in that way." He's looking me right in the eyes as he says this. "Courtney and I are getting along great, you know? And I love her. Probably even more than I should."

I can tell from his expression that he's completely sincere, and I suddenly get embarrassed about thinking—even for a second—that he was flirting with me. He might be cute as hell with his deep-set black eyes and gloriously sexy accent, but all that cute is 100 percent for Courtney.

And what kind of friend am I to think that he'd ever flirt with me—well, flirt and actually mean it—when he has Courtney?

"I know you do, and Courtney loves you too. Totally," I tell him as I pop the lid off my latte to help it cool faster. Well, and to buy myself a few seconds to get my head together. "So why are you worried about it? You don't think they decided to go somewhere and chat after work just because?"

Of course I feel like a total hypocrite as I say this,

because I definitely suspect that's not all there was to it. I have that sixth sense emanating from my gut, telling me there's something odd here. I can just *feel* it. And apparently Mat does too.

"No, this is different." He shoves a hand through his dark hair, then leans back in the chair so it tilts up on its back legs. "You know that Dunkin' Donuts over on Route 126? That's where they were. I was driving by and I noticed Courtney's car in the lot. Scott's red car was parked right next to hers. I mean, you couldn't miss them."

I know what he's getting at without him having to spell it out. No one ever goes to that Dunkin' Donuts. We usually go to the one where Mat works, or to the Starbucks where we are now. Or a million other places.

"They didn't want anyone to hear whatever it was they were talking about," he continues. He's not acting all drama-ish about it, just confused in a very macho, guy-ish way. "I thought maybe they were planning a surprise party for you for getting into Harvard. It was the only reason I could think of for them to be there. But I asked Courtney later—in a

200

very offhanded way—if she was planning to do anything like that, and she said no, she'd just gotten you a gift."

I yank at the neck of my sweater so the necklace pops out.

"That's pretty," he says. "That's what she got you?"

I nod. As I tuck it back in, I say, "So you got worried. When you saw them out and couldn't figure out why, I mean."

"I shouldn't be. And I *wouldn't* be, because I absolutely trust her to not cheat on me, let alone with Scott. But you know, there's a lot of other weird stuff going on with her. Aside from her parents breaking up. She's skipping out on classes and she doesn't tell me first, even in classes we have together. She doesn't talk to you or to Anne like she used to. And . . . *Não sei.* I don't know. It's nothing specific, but when I think about it all together, I'm just gettin' a real bad vibe about things. And so is Anne. She stopped by during my shift one night last week for coffee. She acted like she was just there as a casual thing, but she was grilling me about Courtney the whole time. She didn't come right out and say anything was wrong, but she's obviously worried about Courtney too."

So Anne was busy last week. "Have you asked Courtney about it?"

"Not really." He lets his chair clonk back down onto all four legs. He leans toward me, putting his elbows on the table. "Definitely not about skipping school. You know how defensive she'll probably get."

"Been there, done that. She promised not to do it again, though."

One of his eyebrows cocks up. "Well, that's something, I guess. I did end up asking her flat out about that night she was with Scott. A few days after I saw them, we were on our way to her place and we drove by that same Dunkin' Donuts. So I mentioned seeing her car and Scott's car there. I did it in a way that sounded like it just occurred to me as we were passing by. You know, so she'd know I was curious but so she wouldn't think it was any big thing." He shoots me a lopsided grin before adding, "I left out the part about how I'd made a U-turn in the middle of Route 126 and parked across the street and watched them for ten minutes."

"You didn't!"

"What can I say? With everything that's been going on, I was worried about my woman." He says "my woman" in a lovey way, one that's not derogatory or possessive at all, which makes me like him even more. And makes me think that he really is good for Courtney, even if they did hop into the sack faster than I think is smart.

"So what'd she say about it? Anything?"

He shakes his head. "She claimed they got together to talk about their manager at Stop & Shop. That she's being a real jerk about time cards and a million other things. But it was a lie."

"It was? How do you know?" I feel like a total dork playing dumb about all this, but I'm getting the sinking feeling that Courtney's about to screw up her relationship with Mat even worse than she tried to screw up our friendship that night at Bennigan's. And if Mat ends up breaking up with her over this, she's going to fall apart, and I soooo don't want to have that happen.

"First, she's never once complained about her manager to me, and for all the time we spend together talking, you'd think she'd have said something. At least once. And she also told me a couple other people from work were at the Dunkin' Donuts, too, and they were all discussing the same things. She made it sound like a big get-together."

He sucks in his lower lip, then takes a long sip of coffee, like he's trying to keep himself calm. When he sets his cup down and speaks again, his voice is completely flat. "Jenna, there were only a few other people in that Dunkin' Donuts. And they weren't Stop & Shop types, either. There was this one old couple sitting on the opposite side of the seating area from Courtney and Scott. Everyone else just walked in, stood in line, got their coffee, and left. No one else was talking to them at all."

"Couldn't they have been there already and left?"

Mat shoots me a look. "What do you think?"

"Okay, okay," I say. "But don't read too much into it. And whatever you do, do *not* let your imagination run away with you. Courtney is *not* cheating on you. I swear."

"But it wasn't just a casual coffee, either. Something is going on."

I can't convince him otherwise, so why try? "Yeah, I think something is going on too. But it's not cheating." Despite Courtney telling me about Scott's yum factor.

"Do you know what it is, then? Or is it some deep, dark secret?" He levels a stare at me that makes me want to tell him about what I overheard when I picked Scott up from the store to go bowling. Or all about Scott making up that story about Courtney applying to Syracuse. But what good would it do?

"I have no idea. But like you said, Courtney's my best friend. I have to trust her. And if something's really wrong, we have to hope she'll come to one of us."

But the truth is, I really don't trust her right now—not completely—and I'm not sure I'm convincing Mat that I am. Then a brainstorm hits me. "You know, Scott's parents are divorced, and his dad just remarried. Maybe Courtney feels like she can talk to him about it in a way she can't talk to us. Neither of us have ever had to deal with anything like that."

"Maybe. That hadn't occurred to me." He looks

doubtful, though. Probably because he's thinking that Courtney would be far more likely to talk to Anne about it all.

And now that I think about it, the dead meat comments don't make any more sense in the share-our-misery-over-divorcing-parents context, either.

"If you see or hear anything, will you let me know?" he asks. "If something more serious is going on—something other than her parents' divorce, even if she's breaking up with me for whatever reason— I'd rather know about it and deal with it than constantly be worried about her."

"I will. But really, I think it's not the big thing you think." I hate that I'm making excuses for Courtney, but telling him I'm just as suspicious as he is will make everything worse.

And it really *could* be nothing.

"Let's hope." He finishes the last dregs of his coffee, but leaves the cup on the table while I work on mine. There's something calm and polite about him that I really like, and I can totally see why he rings Courtney's bells. After watching her parents' up-and-down relationship for years, I bet she finds him stabilizing.

"So, what's the plan for tomorrow night?" he asks, clearly ready to put the whole awkward conversation behind us. "Courtney says there's some big party at Aric Jensen's. Scott mentioned it to me too. I think he's all hot to go, but Courtney said she wanted to go to the movies with you. Did you and Scott ever figure it out?"

"Oh, crap! I meant to ask Scott about that." Courtney's gonna kill me if I don't let her know tonight. "I have no clue what we're doing. I want to go to the movies, but I should double check with Scott first."

"He might not be home yet. You wanna try his cell?"

I'm already pulling my phone out of my purse and dialing. When Scott answers, it's obvious he's still in the car. I can hear his radio blasting in the background.

"It's just me," I say. "I forgot to ask: What's the deal tomorrow night? Mat and Courtney are wondering too. Court asked me if I want to go to the movies, and I was thinking—"

"I didn't tell you yet?"

"Nope."

"Hold on a sec." The sound of the car radio fades in the background, then he comes back on the line. "Sorry. Needed to turn that down. I meant to tell you that I told Aric Jensen we'd go to his place, so he's kind of expecting us. I figured that way you can go out with Courtney on Saturday night. I was thinking of going over to the gym for some hoops with the guys then, since they're opening it up for the night. That way, you guys can have your girl time, after everything that's been going on."

"You don't think Aric's will be insane?" I say, even as Mat is pretending to gag on the other side of the table. I shoot Mat a *stop it* kind of grin, then pretend to ignore him as he rolls his eyes.

"Probably, but it'll be fun. And if it's not, then we'll leave. No big deal. Since we missed Rick Dando's and Lucas Ribiero's parties at the beginning of break, we really should show for this one."

I can tell from the way he's talking that he won't change his mind, and since he's encouraging me to go out with Courtney on Saturday and being supportive of what I want, I don't see the point in arguing. "Okay, I'll let Mat and Courtney know so they can make plans. Have a good time learning fiscal responsibility."

"Yeah, right. I'm sure it'll be the most exciting night of my life. I just pulled into the driveway and I can see my mom through the den window. She's all geared up."

"I'm so sorry," I say, trying not to laugh.

"I can tell. Talk to you later, okay?"

I tell him good-bye, then snap the phone shut. Mat's still pretending to gag, so I toss a wadded-up napkin at him. "Apparently the school gym's open for basketball on Saturday night, so he suggested that Courtney and I go to the movies then. It's a good idea, so what was I going to say?"

"That Aric Jensen's a drunk and you don't want to go to his party?"

"It won't be so bad."

Mat takes our two empty cups over to the trash. As he tosses them in, he says, "Nah, it won't be bad. You, me, and Courtney can stick together and we'll be fine. But I just hate these parties where all anyone does is play stupid drinking games or hook up in the bedrooms. It's juvenile."

"College will be worse."

"That's what I'm afraid of."

He pulls his keys out of his pocket, then asks if I'm ready to go. I nod and pull my jacket off the back of the chair. He—get this—takes it out of my hands and helps me into it. I'm not sure if it's dorky or if it's just that he was raised this way. But as we walk out of Starbucks and he opens the door for me, allowing me to go first, I decide it's all pretty cool. "You know, you're all right, Mateus the Great," I tell him, using the name Courtney always calls him. As if he's Alexander or something, out to conquer lands and women's hearts everywhere.

"You thought I wasn't?"

I look sideways at him as we cross the parking lot, and I'm about to say something to cover myself when I see that he's got a teasing grin on his face. "Shut up," I say, and laugh, though when he uses his clicker to unlock the car, I race ahead of him to open my own door before he can do it. Just because.

I hear him laughing as he walks around to his

side of the car. He has confidence in himself that's completely different from the kind of confidence Scott has. Mat's is the kind that other people might not see right away. It's subtle. On the other hand, everyone who meets Scott knows from the get-go that he's the kind of person who runs his own show. Not because he brags about himself or anything; it's just that he has this aura about him he can't hide, even when he's quiet.

"Sorry, but it's snowing," I say once he's sitting in the driver's seat. "No sense in your taking any longer to get into the car than you needed to."

"Yeah, yeah, yeah," he says. He knows the way to my house, since he and Courtney have picked me up several times, so I don't bother giving him directions. When we arrive, he pulls up so my door is right next to the front walk, just so I won't get my feet messy going in. "You want me to get out and open your door for you?"

"Smartass. But thanks for the ride." I grab the handle, but he reaches across and puts a hand on my elbow to stop me.

"Promise me you'll keep an eye on Courtney?"

"I promise."

He squeezes my elbow, then lets go. *"Obrigada por tudo."*

I wave to him from the porch as he backs his decade-old silver Nissan out of the driveway, then watch as he turns down the street, heading for his house. I can't put a finger on why—certainly not because of the weather—but I have a warm and fuzzy feeling inside.

When I get inside and check in with Mom and Dad, it occurs to me that I really meant it when I told him I'd keep an eye on Courtney. He's the kind of guy I want to believe is truly a friend, the kind who'll always have my back. And I want him to know he can rely on me too.

As I climb the stairs, deciding to skip TV (and the endless postholiday reruns) and just go to bed, I realize that my accidental meeting with Mat was probably the chance encounter that was supposed to change my whole day.

Not that I believe in horoscopes.

My horoscope couldn't have been right.

It's two a.m. and I can't sleep, despite having read

an entire *Shape* magazine front to back, followed by an entire *Teen People.* So I'm at the computer, horsing around and doing Google searches on Mount Ida and on Simmons College (just to see where Courtney might go), and trying to bore my brain back into sleep mode.

And as I'm waiting for the Simmons site to load the page describing its various majors, it just hits me: My horoscope said that my Leo partner (namely, Scott) would be testy today. Well, yesterday, since it's after midnight now. But he wasn't testy at all.

I go through my old e-mail just to reread the horoscope. When I find it and click it open, I see that it also said that it isn't the time to simply let my Leo roar, but to get to the root of his problem.

Scott roaring? Definitely not his style, and he has zero problems to roar about, anyway. Well, other than not getting into Harvard, and that's not really a *problem.* He'll get in during the regular cycle.

I hope.

Well, and there's the not-getting-laid problem.

I click out of the horoscope and go back to bed, then lie flat on my back, staring through the dark at the ceiling. Is Scott getting testy about the whole sex thing and I just don't know it?

No, I tell myself as I roll over onto my side. Horoscopes aren't real.

"Are they listening to ABBA in there?" I ask Scott as I get out of the Jetta, then jump over the pile of snow separating the sidewalk from the road near the end of Aric Jensen's driveway.

Scott grabs me around the waist and lifts me into the air, spinning me in a circle over the icy cement. At the top of his lungs he sings, "You are my dancing queen . . ."

"Stop it!"

He lowers me so my feet barely touch the ground, then whispers, "Only seventeen . . ." before he gives me a sweet, warm kiss.

"You are such a goober," I tell him as I take a step backward. I love when he's acting cheery and mischievous like this.

"Hey, I know my ABBA," he says, taking my hand as we start uphill, following the driveway toward the front of Aric's house. "My dad and Amber took me to see *Mamma Mia* when it was in Boston."

I try not to look shocked, but I just can't see Scott dancing in the aisles to ABBA with a bunch of forty- and fifty-somethings.

"I know, I know," he says, swinging my hand as we walk. "But I really had fun. Just don't tell anyone."

"Oh, believe me, I won't," I say as we get to the top of the hill and start up the brick walkway to the front door. I've been here a couple times before, when we were younger and Aric hosted birthday parties or other little kid events. But I haven't been here since we started high school. And I forgot how friggin' enormous his house is. A total McMansion, complete with soaring arched windows, evergreens covered in Christmas lights on either side of the walkway, and a double-wide oak front door that's polished to a high shine. We walk in without ringing, because it's obvious that the party's in full swing and no one inside can hear the doorbell over the music and all the talking, anyway.

There's a den off to the right as we go in, where tons of coats are piled on top of what I assume has to be a sofa. I shrug out of my coat and try to find a place on the pile where I can toss it without the entire mountain coming down on my feet.

"Here." Scott takes my coat, then nods toward the other side of the hallway. I follow him through the crowd in the entry hall—mostly walking sideways and trying not to bump anyone or spill their drinks—until we come out in the living room. There are quite a few people here, too, but moving is much easier. Scott walks through to the dining room, then points to a small space between the china cabinet and an outside wall that is occupied by a gigantic potted plant. "I'm going to fold our coats and tuck them down here, behind the plant. They're a lot less likely to get taken or spilled on here."

"Just remember where they are at the end of the night," I tell him. This house is so big, I'm afraid I won't remember which plant in which room is the one hiding our coats.

"No worries," Scott says. He puts his hands on either side of my waist to give me a quick kiss, then turns it into more. I let him because I'm just picking up the best vibe from him. Something that makes me think he's here because he wants to be with me and to show me off, not because he wants to hang with the guys or drink like a fish or get an ego boost from all the girls who drool after him, which is what I've been worried about ever since he said he wanted to come here tonight. Something that makes me want to blow off whatever it is he and Courtney have been talking about, and just enjoy the night.

Plus, his kisses are freaking amazing.

When he finally lets me go, he has a smile on his face that lights me up inside. "I want you to have fun tonight. It's our last night together before school starts again Monday. I want it to be special. The best New Year's ever."

"Me too," I tell him. "Just don't forget to kiss me at midnight."

"Oh, don't worry about that. I've got it all planned out."

"You do, do you?"

He grins, then leads me out of the dining room with his hand resting on the small of my back. I glance at him over my shoulder. "Where to?"

"Let's go in the kitchen, grab a drink, and then see what's what."

"Courtney and Mat should be here already," I tell him, though I have to raise my voice and lean back so my mouth is close to his ear to be heard. "She told me they were going to be here at nine, and it's almost ten."

"I'll keep my eyes open," he says. "We should try to say hi to Aric before he gets too smashed. And I need to talk to some of the guys to see what time we're meeting up for hoops tomorrow night."

"Who are you playing with?"

"Just some guys from the team," he says with a shrug. "We totally sucked against Wellesley two weeks ago and we play them again right after break, so Coach Ritter wants us to run through some pick-and-roll drills. We really screwed up our inbounding in that game too. Completely inexcusable."

He starts talking about how some guy on the Wellesley team is six feet six, but how they think they can get around him. I'm just smiling and nodding, because—in addition to all the party noise making it hard to hear him—I only vaguely get basketball. I mean, I understand the basics and I love going out and shooting hoops just for fun, but the logistics of actual plays are beyond me. At this point,

I'm not going to ask Scott to explain the definition of a "pick-and-roll." It'd be too humiliating to let on that I have no clue what he's talking about.

We finally make it to the Jensens' enormous kitchen, and it's the exact opposite of my parents' tacky-but-cozy 1980s kitchen. This one's modern, with stainless-steel appliances and shining black granite countertops. There's not a thing on any of the counters either. No toaster, no flour or sugar canisters, nothing. It's like someone came through and sanitized it all. Well, except for the three little ceramic plaques hanging from ribbons beside the sink, each with a different Bible verse.

"Hey, man!" I nearly fall over as Aric Jensen comes up behind us and stumbles into Scott. "I was wonderin' when you'd get here. Where the hell is your beer?"

"Dude, you didn't bring me one?" Scott says as he and Aric knock their closed fists together in greeting.

"Hell, I can barely walk. The keg got here at seven." He points toward the far end of the kitchen, and sure enough, there's a keg surrounded by a group of juniors and seniors. "I think we're almost out of cups, though. Here"—he ducks around the kitchen island and, after making sure no one's looking, grabs two red plastic cups out of a bottom cabinet—"from the emergency stash. Have at it."

"Thanks, man." Before I can tell Scott I'd prefer to just grab a soda from the fridge, he's across the room and elbowing his way to the tap.

Aric reaches over and flips the end of one of my curls. "Hey, glad you could make it, brainiac. Guess now that you're into Harvard, you can let go of some of your anal-retentive tendencies and make it to one of my parties, huh?"

I'm about to say something sarcastic, but I realize from his expression that he's actually being complimentary. "Yeah. Scott's been on me to get out more. Thanks for inviting us."

"Well, I think it rocks that you got into Harvard. And you *should* be out celebrating." The edge of his mouth curves up and he says, "Scott probably shit a brick when you got in and he didn't. He'll get in on the next round, though. Hell, if I can get into MIT—"

"You got into MIT?" I know I sound surprised,

but I had no idea Aric was even thinking about MIT, let alone that he might have good enough grades to get in. Not that I think he lacks the ability—he's always struck me as being fairly smart—but he's definitely not one of those guys who competes in Brain Bowl or hangs out at the computer lab after school.

"Yeah. Just got the letter yesterday." A blush creeps into his cheeks, and he takes a long sip of his beer—I assume to hide the fact he's embarrassed. He sets his cup on the counter and adds, "I lucked out on the SATs, and my dad got me a job with a biotech company in Cambridge last summer so I could get some good recs and have something to say in my interview. But don't go telling everyone. Might ruin my rep."

"Your secret is safe with me."

He smiles, then says, "Thanks. But I did want to tell you congrats on Harvard. And that I'll cross my fingers for Scott to get in too."

He looks past me, toward the monstrous family room, where someone is flipping channels on a flat-screen television that takes up half of the far wall. "I don't see her now, but Courtney Delahunt was looking for you," Aric says. "About a half hour ago."

"Is she still around?"

"She was in the family room when I saw her, over by the couch. She was with her boyfriend—the Brazilian guy, I think his name's Mat?—anyway, I heard him tell her she should go outside and try to call you on your cell, but I'm not sure if she did."

"Thanks. I'll try to find her." His eyes are a little red, but despite his claim that he can barely walk and the boisterous way he greeted Scott, he looks sober enough to be able to tell a half hour from an hour.

"If I see her before you do, I'll let her know that you and Scott are here."

"Thanks."

I turn to go find Scott, but Aric puts a hand on my arm. "Hey, Jenna?"

I stop and look at him. There's just something in his tone that sounds very un-Aric-like.

"You know, I'm not exactly Courtney's favorite person." He brushes what looks like potato chip crumbs off the front of his shirt, then shrugs. "We get along all right and all, but . . . well, she doesn't exactly make a point of finding me at a party to say hey—you know?"

"Do you think she went home?"

"No, that's not my point. It's just . . . when she didn't see you around, she pushed her way through the whole party to find me and ask about you. And I picked up a really weird vibe from her."

I frown at him. "Weird how?"

"I don't know, exactly. Just weird. She really seemed worried about you. And she was asking about Scott, too. Like she was afraid you guys might've ditched her and gone to a different party or something." I can tell he's dying of curiosity but trying to sound like he doesn't really care as he asks, "Is everything okay?"

"With Courtney? Or with me and Scott?"

"Both, I guess."

I shrug. "As far as I know, everything's good."

Well, except for Aric Jensen asking me if everything's okay. *That* is weird. Weird enough to make me wonder if there really is something going on.

Then again, I had no clue he was the MIT type either.

"Well, have a good time tonight, okay?" His voice is low and serious. Like he's afraid I'm about to have a stress-induced heart attack right here in his kitchen and it's his duty to prevent it. "You did it, Jenna. You're in. So go dance and drink and don't worry about anything tonight."

Chapter

10

I scan the mass of people dancing in the family room, trying to pick out Courtney's blond hair and not think too much about Aric Jensen.

Courtney's always been right about one thing: I am a horrible judge of character. I mean, how shallow am I that I've always judged Aric based on gossip about his wild parties rather than on his brains? Or on actual conversations I've had with him in the years since, I dunno, fourth or fifth grade?

How bad can the guy be if he's smart enough to get into MIT, modest enough to not brag about it, and caring enough to worry about Courtney finding me?

As I watch the crowd move around me and listen to them all sing along with the music and greet one another with huge grins on their faces, I feel a pang of envy. Clearly, Aric's learned to balance his social life and his school life better than I have. There's no way I'd have been able to get into a good school—probably any school—if I partied the way Aric does. I know the trade-off was worth it for me, but for the first time, I resent that some people didn't have to make the trade-off at all.

I take a few steps into the family room, staying within eyesight of the keg so Scott can find me, while at the same time trying to see farther into the room.

A few seconds later Aric passes by me and grabs the ass of a skinny but well-endowed junior, then offers to get her a beer while she lets out a completely fake giggle.

I try to look past them. Maybe I shouldn't try to guess a thing about anyone. Just keep reminding myself that I need to live my life for me and not give a fly about what other people are doing with theirs.

"Hey, Jenna! There you are!" I hear Courtney, barely, over the music thumping from the speakers and turn to look to my right, in the general direction of her voice.

She scoots between a group of guys who are talking with their hands—right in the middle of all the people who are trying to dance—and a couple who've decided to make out. When she finally makes it to me, after nearly having her head knocked off by one of the hand-talkers, she yells, "I just tried to call you on your cell!"

"Like I could hear it ring." I jiggle my purse, which is lying flat against my hip, hanging from a strap I've looped diagonally across my body to keep from losing it in the crowd. "I can't believe how loud it is in here!"

"I know!" She looks incredible—her hair is piled on her head in a style I know took her a while to do, but that looks casual and thrown-together in a very sexy way. And she's wearing The Skirt. I'm about to compliment her, but she leans in close to me and says, "When'd you get here? Did you know I've been looking all over for you? And where's Scott?"

"About ten or fifteen minutes, Aric told me, and Scott's getting me a drink," I answer, tackling her questions one by one. "I told you we probably wouldn't get here until close to ten. What's the problem?"

"No problem," she says, but I can tell it's a lie. Her words are coming out too fast. "It's just that since you missed Rick Dando's and Lucas Ribiero's parties, I was afraid you might not show up here. I thought Scott might take you somewhere else. Or something."

It's the first time she's mentioned the fact Scott and I skipped out on them after Bennigan's. But rather than acting hurt or pissed off, she simply sounds relieved to know I'm here tonight.

She gets bumped from behind by a senior who's dancing with way too much enthusiasm given how many people are crammed into the room. Courtney just rolls her eyes. "You're not staying too long, are you? I know how much you hate stuff like this. Maybe we can all go somewhere."

"Scott wants to stay until midnight so we don't miss the countdown," I tell her. "I can live with the noise till then. It's the first party we've been to all of break, and it's important to him."

Courtney looks past me, and I turn to see Scott walking up, two beers in hand. He gives one to me, then says hello to Courtney and asks about Mat.

"Bathroom," she says, then wrinkles her nose. "Piece of advice? If either of you need to go, use the one upstairs by Aric's parents' room. The one down here is nearly out of toilet paper."

"I think I'm good," I say, trying not to laugh, because it's such a typical Courtney warning. "I came prepared. If you need any tissue, tell me."

"And guys don't care," Scott adds.

"True," she says. She glances at my cup, then her head jerks up. A typical person would never recognize it, but I see a definite pissedness in her gaze as she turns to Scott. "You got her a *beer*?"

"Chill, Courtney," he shoots back, a definite edge to his voice. "It's not a crime."

"Actually, it is a crime," she says, right as I'm thinking the exact same thing. But I wasn't going to say it, though, and I'm stunned that Court did.

"I'm only having one, then I'm switching to

Coke," I tell her, hoping to diffuse whatever is up between the two of them. Although, as I take a tiny sip, I figure I probably won't even finish this one. It's not that I'm worried about getting plowed—I know I can handle one or two beers just fine—but I'm really not in the mood to drink. And frankly, I *do* worry about getting caught. A lot.

I look over my shoulder at Scott, who puts one hand on my lower back, then raises his plastic cup to his lips for a long swig. "And you'd better have only one too," I tell him. "You're my designated driver."

"You got it, baby." He leans in and kisses me on my neck, right below my jawline. "You two gonna be okay if I go find the guys? I gotta figure out the basketball thing. Then let's dance. It's New Year's Eve, and I plan to celebrate big."

"We're more than okay," Courtney says. "Just find us when you're done."

When Scott walks away, I can't help but ask Courtney, "What in the world is up with you two lately?"

Her eyes crinkle at the corners, which is a classic

move when she's about to pretend something's inconsequential that's not. "Whaddya mean?"

"You and Scott." I take a long drink of my beer, figuring the sooner I get it down and move on to soda, the better. "You two are acting all annoyed with each other lately."

"What have I told you about trying to read people?" She tilts her head toward the kitchen to indicate that we should head that way, and I edge through the crowd as she finds a path for us. Once we're near the counter, where we can actually hear each other without shouting, she says, "There's nothing 'up' with me and Scott, and I'm not annoyed with him. Seriously. He's probably just crabby about my saying that I wanted to skip Aric's party, you know? Not a big deal."

She's trying not to look down at the beer in my hand while she says all this, so I explain: "He went to get it before I could tell him I didn't want it."

"So don't drink it."

"I don't want to hurt his feelings." Even as the words are leaving my mouth, though, it dawns on me that while I'm supposedly doing my best to live my life the way I want—trying not to take other people's opinions to heart, not having sex with Scott until I'm ready, trying not to tell Courtney how to live her life or let her decisions affect me—I'm totally cheating at it. Doing things like coming to Aric's party and drinking this stupid, nasty-tasting beer as a bass-ackwards way of making it up to Scott for not having sex with him. Which, of course, I haven't even had the guts to tell him yet—I mean, that it's not just going to be a while so I can try to relax. But that it could be a *long* while. And that I don't want to relax. Well, not that way.

I swish the beer in the cup and stare down at the golden liquid. I am such a chickenshit.

I take one more swig, then dump the end of the beer down the sink. I turn back to Courtney and say, "Since Scott's not here, I guess I shouldn't worry about his feelings."

"Want me to pour you some soda?"

I open the cupboard under the sink, guessing that's where the garbage must be (and it is), then toss in my cup. "Nah. Let's go dance."

I need to do something that *I* want to do, and

Courtney and I always have a blast when we're dancing. Dancing also means I don't have to talk to her too much. I'm still feeling a little uncomfortable with her and I don't want to get into any serious conversations until I've sorted out my emotions and can stop being such a wuss.

Plus, I'm feeling energized. Loose. I know there's no way my piddly little half a beer is affecting me so fast, but I can feel my heart rate picking up, and it's like my feet have a life of their own, pulling me back toward the family room. A fast dance tune is on, and more people are moving from the front hall and the kitchen toward the music.

"Cool mix, huh?" Courtney says as we move through the room, trying to find a space open enough to really dance. "You missed some good songs earlier."

"But you're here now, and that's what counts," Mat says, surprising me and Courtney by popping out of the crowd near us. "You two were coming in here to dance with me, right?"

"Absolutely!" I don't know what's with me, but I suddenly feel like I really, really need to dance. Like someone's shot my veins full of adrenaline and I have to work it out of my system. I see an open spot and push toward it, then nearly trip when I realize that's where someone put the coffee table.

"Sorry," I mumble to the group of people who are huddled on the floor around it, bouncing quarters off its smooth surface into a tall red plastic cup full of beer. I feel like a total dork, but then someone else bumps into the table from the other side—apparently thinking the same thing I did, that they'd discovered a few open feet of dance space.

"Um, maybe you oughta move the table?" I tell the guy nearest me as he grabs the quarter and prepares to send it pinging toward the cup.

This brings a bunch of groans and eye-rolling and one "Maybe you oughta just watch where you're going."

"Jen, you okay?" Courtney says, pulling me away, toward another semi-open spot.

"Yeah. Great!" I let out a little whoop as my absolute favorite eighties song comes on. Who'da guessed Aric Jensen would have such wild taste in music? "Just dance with me!"

Mat maneuvers his body to get us all a little more

dancing space, and we start moving to the music. I just close my eyes, let my body go, and have fun. Forget all about the jerks with their quarters table. Forget all about Scott and school, and about my minor flip-out at the hotel. Forget about Mark's e-mails, my wonky horoscopes, and all about Courtney. I just go with how I feel.

I don't know why, but a couple great songs later, I'm suddenly feeling totally light-headed and spacey, like I'm drunk. Even though I know I can't possibly be.

Maybe Scott was right. I *need* to get out and relax. At least a little.

I must look it, too, because I'm mid-groove when Mat yells, "Hey, Jenna! You okay?"

"I told you guys, I feel great!" Though I'm starting to wonder. Mat's voice sounded like it was coming out of an echo chamber. Distant.

They look at each other, shrug, and keep dancing. And I swear, if I wasn't feeling so loopy, I'd think Courtney looked guilty.

But like she says, I am soooooo not a good judge of people. So whhaaaat-ever.

I just grin at them, letting the music pound through my head and move my hips and my hands. I decide to think about how good I look in my new, low-slung black pants. And how my pink wraparound shirt makes me look like I actually have boobs. And I think about how next year I'm going to be at Harvard. Going to parties with Harvard kids. And hopefully getting some kick-ass grades.

As I'm mentally singing along with the music, I hear Scott's voice in my head, singing right along with me. I open my eyes, and he's right there, dancing with us. "Courtney and Mat got you dancing," he says, his eyes full of amusement.

"Hey, I got *them* dancing," I say. Just as the words are out of my mouth, I feel someone's chest connecting straight on with my back, and I start to fall forward.

"Watch out!" Scott reaches behind me to push a guy I vaguely recognize from the basketball team off of me.

He gives Scott a slow, bleary smile. "Hey, Bannister. Sorry, man. Didn't mean to fall on your girlfriend." The tall redhead looks down at me and adds,

"Sorry, Scott's girlfriend," before making his way past us, toward the coffee table.

I shouldn't find it funny, but I do. And I can't stop giggling. And then I get the feeling I'm gonna hurl.

"You did it, didn't you?" I hear Courtney say.

I quit laughing long enough to look at her, but I can't quite focus on her face. There are black spots in the way, and I can't make my brain wrap around them to see properly. "Do what?"

"I didn't do jack," Scott says.

"What are you talking about?" Mat asks, but Courtney's totally ignoring him. She's glaring at Scott like he just murdered someone.

"Get off my case, Courtney. She's fine." He wraps his arms around my waist from behind, spreading his hands across my stomach. "She had a beer for once in her life."

"Beer, my ass!"

He rests his chin on my shoulder and whispers in my ear, "Ignore her. You're good—right, baby?"

I nod, even though I don't think I'm so good at all. My mouth isn't working. Or maybe I don't want it to work. 'Cause Courtney looks like she's ready to rip someone's head off. Instead, she grabs me so hard, she nearly rips my arm off. "Come on, Jenna. We've gotta get out of here."

"No way," Scott says, pulling me back against him, hard. I start to protest—mainly because I'm trying to use every ounce of my energy not to yak up my dinner—but Scott doesn't even hear me. He's too busy trying to take Courtney's fingers off my arm, even though she's refusing to let go.

"You're delusional, Courtney!" Scott yells. "And I'm sick of you trying to run Jenna's life."

"She's sick!"

"Then *I'll* take her home," Scott says. He starts pushing me toward the door. I let him. I can't deal with either of them right now. I'm more worried about how half a beer has me ready to pass out.

Maybe the salmon Mom made for dinner wasn't cooked or something. Maybe I should call her. See if she and Dad are sick. I fumble for my purse, but it drops to the ground as I'm trying to get the strap over my head.

Dammit.

Scott's still pushing me toward the door, and I don't have the energy to push back to get my purse. When I manage to look up, I realize we're in the dining room. Scott lets me go, bending down behind the plant to get our coats.

"I picked this up for you." Mat's voice comes to me as if it's floating through the air so slowly, I can actually see the sound. I feel him loop my purse back over my shoulder, and then jolt as Scott starts yelling at Mat, and Mat actually yells back.

I can't seem to follow what they're saying. Only that it's loud. And that Scott wants me to come with him, and Mat's saying I shouldn't and telling me I need to choose.

"Courtney?" I hear myself ask. But it sounds hideous. Like a whine. And then I'm moving backward, away from all their voices. Scott's voice is angry. Very angry. Then I feel a whoosh of cold air as a door opens in front of me and I realize I'm on the sidewalk.

It's like I floated here.

I think I'm going to miss the New Year's countdown.

Just as I manage to ask what time it is, I bring up

the nastiness in my stomach. One huge urp into the beautiful evergreens with their white, sparkling Christmas lights. I take a deep breath of the winter air and force myself to focus.

I only had half a beer. This doesn't happen from half a beer. How did this happen?

I fight down a wave of panic. This is all wrong. Very, very wrong.

Why won't my brain work? Why can't I make it move from point A to point B, and figure out why I'm in such rough shape? And what I need to do to feel better?

"Come on, Jen, I've got you." It's Courtney. I don't see Scott or Mat, but since I can barely see Courtney, I'm not sure who's with me and who's not. I'm too freaking dizzy to try to look. It's like the sidewalk under me is moving, which is not a good thing when it's so icy out.

Then I start vomiting like I've never vomited in my life. So hard it hurts my eyes, making me wonder if I'm going to pop a blood vessel. "Help," I manage as I gasp for air.

"I'm taking you to the hospital," I hear Courtney

say, and then I feel arms holding me up. I try to argue—I want her help, but I want Scott, too, and I don't want to choose—but I can't. I can't string together the words to form a sentence.

Oh, crap. My parents are going to get called if I go to the hospital. They are going to be really, really pissed.

"How much alcohol was in her system?"

I can't open my eyes. I'm tired, and it's just too difficult. But the voice is my mother's, and she sounds so calm, I know instantly that things are serious.

I'm so sorry, Mom. I think it. I can't say it.

"I don't believe alcohol is the issue," another voice answers. I don't recognize this one. It's male. Older.

"She only had one beer," Courtney's voice comes from somewhere nearby. Is she sitting next to me? "And I saw her pour part of it out. She just wanted to dance."

There's a pause. I think someone says something, but then I hear Courtney say, "I swear, Mrs. Kassarian. Jenna's not a drinker. I don't think I've ever seen her drink before. She wasn't going to the party tonight to drink. Really."

I feel like I need to say something, to tell Mom that Courtney's telling the truth. That she can believe in me. That I'm still the same good kid I've always been. But I'm completely frozen. Exhausted all the way through to my bones. And I'm not even certain I'm hearing the whole conversation. Pieces seem to be missing.

Wait, am I in a hospital? I vaguely remember Courtney saying something about taking me to the hospital.

"What do you believe *is* the issue?" My mom's all business, making it clear she's going to deal with my health first, and with Courtney and the whole beer issue later.

"Have you ever heard of date rape drugs?" It's the man again.

"You believe someone put a drug in her drink?"

"It's possible. We'd like to run some tests. There are several different types, but we've seen an uptick in cases involving GHB, a certain type of date rape drug, in this part of Massachusetts in recent months." The man's voice keeps fading in and out—I can't focus on the words—but I hear him mention something about classic symptoms, and then he says there are a few other drugs that might have caused me to get so sick. And I hear the word "roofie." That sometimes people who aren't aware of its dangers treat it like a recreational drug, thinking it'll simply help them relax.

My stomach lets out a gurgle that's unmistakable. I feel someone—a nurse?—help me onto my side, and then I vomit again. I think there's a bin. I'm not sure.

I feel like I have the worst case of the flu I've ever had. I'm dog-tired, and even though I can tell I'm not going to vomit anymore, I don't want to eat anything either.

I just want to sleep. I want it all to go away. And I want the doctor and my parents to stop asking me questions I can't answer.

"Hey."

I glance toward the door of my hospital room and see Courtney standing there. She's in different clothes—The Skirt has given way to her favorite pair of faded Levi's and an Old Navy T-shirt—and her hair is back to her everyday style.

"Hey, yourself," I say. I blink a couple times, realizing that the sun's all the way up now. It's probably noon or later. And I'm thinking, *Happy New Year, idiot.* As in, *How could I start what's supposed to be one of the best years of my life doing something so stupid?*

She hesitates, then comes to sit beside me. "How are you feeling?"

"Bright and perky," I say in my most sarcastic voice. "Like I'm ready to run the Boston Marathon."

She gets a look like I slapped her. "Come on, Jen."

I force down a sigh. "Honestly?"

"Honestly."

"I feel awful. I can't believe some jerk slipped me a roofie at Aric's. You know that's what the doctor told my mom that the blood and urine tests showed, right? That I had Rohypnol in my system? I should've known not to drink any beer. I wonder if anyone else got sick."

"No, just you." She leans back in the chair, fiddling with a piece of fuzz on the mauve cushion. "And it's not your fault. It's mine."

"How is it *your* fault?"

She looks up at the ceiling. Her eyes are filled with regret and fear, and I can tell she's trying to hold back tears. "Because that roofie never would've gotten in your drink if it wasn't for me."

Chapter

11

She starts to say something else, then shuts up pronto when a nurse wearing a cotton, floral-patterned top and dusty blue pants comes in, acting all chipper and asking me things like, "How are we doing today?" as if I'm a plural.

Another one of my pet peeves: I hate when people say "we" when they really mean "you." And the fact that I want to rip the truth out of Courtney, which I can't do with Miss Nicey Nurse in the room, makes the nurse's "we" comment piss me off even more than it usually would.

Nicey Nurse rolls a small table next to my bed, then walks back into the hall and returns immediately with a blue plastic tray, which she deposits onto the rolling table. There's milk, water, broth, crackers, and a small bowl of what I think must be vanilla pudding, though the pudding has a very fake yellow cast to it. It reminds me of the pudding they served us at summer camp when we were kids, right out of generically labeled, industrial-size cans.

I hated that pudding.

"Try to get some of this down," Nicey says. I try to focus on what she's saying instead of on the blinding flowers on her top. Why do nurses always have to wear such ugly outfits? What happened to those starched white dresses you see on old television shows? The hats were stupid, but at least the colors weren't painful.

"I'm sure you still feel awful," she says, "but it's because there's nothing in that stomach of yours. If you eat a little something, though, then we can take out the IV this afternoon."

"We can" in this case meaning "she can," take out the IV, I imagine. I can't picture us ripping the thing out together. I mean, I can't even look at my hand right now, which is where the line from the IV drip disappears under a bandage meant to hold the needle in place.

I hate needles. Especially thick needles that have to stay put.

When she finally leaves, I roll my eyes. Courtney wrinkles her nose in the nurse's direction, then gets up and shuts the door.

"So we have some warning next time," she says. "Plus, your parents said they'd be back soon, and we need to talk without them popping in."

I wait for her to explain her comment about the whole roofie thing being her fault, but instead she asks if I'm going to eat anything.

I shoot her the evil eye, but she says, "I know it's nasty. But maybe the crackers will be okay. And it'll mean you can get that needle outta your hand. That looks painful."

"It's more the idea of it that's painful. Painful is my head. And my stomach."

Reluctantly, I pull myself up enough to grab the cracker packet. The effort wears me out, though, and

Courtney takes the packet from me and rips open the plastic.

"I'm just beat. I don't think I've ever been so tired in my entire life." I nod in the direction of the crackers. "Thanks for doing that."

"You won't thank me in a minute."

She waits until she's sure I can eat the crackers on my own, then rolls the table closer so I can reach the straw for the water without having to raise my head too much. When I've got it, she plunks back in the mauve chair.

"So. The roofie." She bites her lip even as she says the word "roofie." "The thing is, I kind of knew about it ahead of time."

Ex-queeze me? "Please tell me you're kidding. I mean, how could you know something like that?"

"It's a long story, but—"

"But you're going to tell me all of it." Or I'll kill her. Once I find the energy.

"You're not going to like it." She looks like she's going to get up and run. But I decide I'll force myself to get out of bed and fall on her if it'll keep her here.

In the most calm, reassuring voice I can muster, I

say, "Just tell me. Please. I promise to listen first and kill you later."

She nods, then gets up and starts walking toward the door. I'm about to yell after her when I realize she's just checking to make sure no one's standing outside, trying to listen. When she gets back, she sits on the side of the bed instead of in the chair. "The police were here earlier, so you never know."

"The police?" How much have I missed?

"Yeah. I'll get to that part."

She'd better. If I'm about to be busted for underage drinking, I'd better know before they come back. Just so I can prepare myself.

Her voice is quiet, and I can barely hear her as she explains: "The night before you and Scott went bowling, I overheard him talking to one of the guys working out on the dock. You know, one of the guys whose job it is to unload the milk trucks."

"He's introduced me to a couple of them," I say. "They seem like mostly nice guys. Scott likes to hang out back on the loading docks when he's on breaks, instead of in the break room."

"All the time," she agrees. "Fresh air and all that.

So, anyway, when I saw him back there at the beginning of break, I wasn't really paying attention to what he was doing. I was just trying to find one of the deli guys who'd gone out for a smoke. Then, all of a sudden, something this one guy was saying to Scott caught my attention."

"Like?"

"He was offering to sell Scott some kind of drug."

I must look doubtful, because Courtney puts her hand on my arm. "Hear me out, okay? I couldn't believe it either. We both know Scott would never do anything to harm his perfect jock bod, right? But instead of telling the guy to blow, Scott started asking how strong it was, and was the guy sure it wasn't dangerous, and it became more and more obvious to me that this was a serious deal and that Scott was totally into it. I totally freaked out. I mean, neither of them had seen me, and I didn't know what to do, so I just turned around and went back in the store."

Courtney's eyes are filling with tears, and even though I have the urge to grab her hand and comfort her, I don't. I want her to tell me the rest.

I also want to know whom to believe here. Because

I'm guessing Scott's story isn't going to be the same as what she's about to tell me, and she hasn't had the best track record for honesty lately. "So did you say anything to him later?" She must've, at some point.

She swallows hard and nods. "When my shift was over, I asked him if he was busy, and when he said no, I told him to meet me after work. That it was really important for us to talk."

"The Dunkin' Donuts on Route 126?"

Her eyebrows arch up in surprise. "How'd you—? I guess Mat told you?"

When I tell her that's where I heard it, she says, "I had to lie to Mat about the whole thing, which was awful. But I felt trapped. Scott made me promise not to tell anyone."

He *made* her? I decide to let it go for the moment, and ask, "So what happened at Dunkin' Donuts?"

"I told Scott what I overheard. At first, he told me I was dreaming—that it couldn't have been him, or that maybe I misunderstood—but he knew he was busted."

"So he never admitted to anything."

"Actually, he did." For a split second, she looks proud of herself, like a TV cop who just got a confession out of a suspect, but the look disappears quickly, and she's serious again. "I wouldn't let up on him, so he eventually admitted that he did talk to the guy about drugs. He even told me it was about roofies—which I hadn't overheard—but that he didn't buy any. And he claimed they weren't for him, anyway. He told me this lame story about how he was curious 'cause someone on the basketball team had been asking him if he knew anything about roofies: what they did, how strong they were, that kind of thing. I told Scott flat out that I didn't believe him. And I told him I was going to tell you and let *you* ask him about it if he didn't feel like he could be honest with me."

I can't say anything. My mouth simply won't move. I cannot even imagine Courtney and Scott having this conversation.

"At that point, we really got into it," she continues, though she keeps glancing at the door as if she's afraid of being caught telling me all this. "We weren't yelling or anything—we were actually pretty quiet—but it was so intense, I was afraid the guy working the Dunkin' Donuts counter was going to come over and check on us to see if we were all right. Anyway, Scott finally admitted everything."

Court's starting to look more and more pissed off as she talks, but what really freaks me out is that I'm starting to believe her. Even when everything I know about Scott is telling me it can't be true, everything I know about Courtney—her expression, the way she can tell things about people, the fact she's been my best friend forever, everything—tells me it *is* true.

"Scott was just so freaking clueless," she says, brushing cracker crumbs off my hospital bed and onto the linoleum. "When he finally got around to telling me the truth, he said it all came up because he'd told the guy working the dock that he was going out with a girl—you—and that you guys hadn't done it yet. That you loved each other and had decided to sleep together, but that you just couldn't relax enough to do it or something. The truck guy told Scott that if it was just a matter of getting you calmed down about it, a roofie—or even half a roofie—would do the trick. That it would relax you, get you turned on. All that crap. And Scott totally bought everything the slimeball said. He was so unbelievably clueless. And I told him so. I told him how dangerous roofies are and that it was *so* not the right way to get you to relax, *if* that was the only problem. Which I didn't believe either. I mean, I know we've talked about how much you love Scott and all, but—"

"I can't believe this—"

"Believe it. I told Scott that if I thought he was even *considering* going back to that truck guy and buying any, that I'd personally find a way to kick his ass and I'd tell you without even blinking, even if I thought you'd break up with him."

"You? Kicking Scott's ass?"

One side of her mouth jerks up. "You know, I was just so pissed, I probably could've. And I wanted to get it through his head that he was being stupid."

It almost all makes sense. But not quite. "So why didn't you ever tell me? Especially if you were so pissed off and worried and whatnot?"

"I didn't think he'd do it once I told him how

dangerous it could be. I mean, Scott's theoretically *smart*." She looks past me, toward a cheesy, framed print on the hospital wall. "But that's not the real reason I didn't say anything. I mean, I was going to tell you even though I didn't think he'd do it, because I still thought you oughta be warned. But he threatened to rat me out for shoplifting if I did. He said he'd tell everyone, and that they'd believe him over me, whether I'd actually done it or not." She stands up and jams her hands into her hair on either side of her head. She's looking away from me, toward the window.

I try to push myself up to a better sitting position, even though it's hard. I can't believe I'm so *tired*. "He accused you of shoplifting?"

She lets her hands fall from her hair, then turns around to face me. "Yeah. And I totally panicked. I wasn't sure until right that minute whether you suspected I'd been stealing stuff. But when he said that, I realized that you did suspect, and that you'd told Scott about it. It hit me how pissed you had to be after that night at Bennigan's, and I was scared to death that I'd lost your friendship forever."

I want to tell her that she'd never lose my friendship, but when I think back, I realize that she was probably right. We hadn't talked in days at that point, and I was still ticked off.

"Scott knew things were bad between us then," she says. "He knew you wouldn't trust anything I said, and he told me so. And just to make sure I wouldn't tell you, he threatened to tell Mat that I'd stolen the nail polish. And the skirt. And your necklace. He said he knew Mat would believe him over me, and I was afraid he would."

"So did you?"

"Steal the stuff?"

I just look at her. She inhales sharply, then slowly lets it out. "I stole the nail polish. And another time, when I was alone, I stole a couple packs of gum at Stop & Shop. And the skirt. The skirt was the biggie. But that's it. I didn't steal the necklace or anything else."

"But why?" The question comes out sounding more harsh than I mean it, but it's because I can barely keep my eyes open. I wonder if it's an aftereffect of the roofie, or if it's something they put in my IV.

"I don't know. Just because, I suppose. The adrenaline rush of getting away with something. Of having a secret. It was stupid. And then I had to lie to cover it up, and it felt awful." She blinks back tears, then says, "I wish I could explain it, but I can't. But I'm sorry, Jenna. I'm really sorry. For lying at Bennigan's, and then at your house when we swapped Christmas gifts, when I lied to cover the Bennigan's lie."

I'm completely blown away by all of this. "I don't know what to say. I mean, you're telling me you stole stuff, but to forgive you, and that my boyfriend used drugs to try to rape me and that you could've stopped it. And that I'm supposed to believe you about everything."

A tear runs down her cheek, and she swipes it away with the back of her hand. "I would never put it that way, but in a nutshell, yeah. I stole, I'm sorry, and your boyfriend—a guy I really, really liked until a couple weeks ago—is a total asshole. And it's about time you knew it. Even if you hate me forever for saying it. Even if you don't believe a word out of my mouth."

Even though the door's shut, we can hear noises out in the hall. "That's probably the police," Courtney says. "I think they were hoping to talk to you about what you remember from Aric's party."

"Did they talk to you already?"

Courtney nods. "Yeah. And I told them everything. About the roofies, about Scott. And even about me stealing and him blackmailing me with it."

My chest suddenly feels like someone's sitting on it. I can hardly breathe as I ask, "Are they going to arrest Scott? Or *you*?"

"I don't know. They might." She lets out a sigh, then walks back to my bed and sits beside me. "I had to do it. I had to tell them. It was the right thing to do even if it means you don't want to be my friend anymore. And if you don't, I'll understand."

She looks at me for a long second, and I try to put my thoughts in some sort of rational order. How can this all be happening? How can I be forced to choose between believing my best friend and my boyfriend?

A memory comes back to me from the party. Of Scott trying to grab my coat from behind the planter. Of his not wanting anyone else to help me.

And I remember hearing my own voice, calling for Courtney.

She breaks her gaze, then starts to stand up from the hospital bed, but I grab her hand and hold it, waiting until she sits back down.

And when she looks at me again, I remember every word of the conversation I overheard at Stop & Shop. And how Courtney said at the end, *I swear, Scott, I'll tell her. I'll tell everyone. And I don't care what you do to me.*

And it all makes sense now.

"You'll always be my friend. My best friend." And I mean it.

I can hardly lift my arms to hug her, so I just let her hug me. And I try not to cry. At least too hard.

Or to think about Scott and the fact he might go to jail. The fact that our relationship is all shot to hell. That I'm going to have to tell the police things I never want to talk about again.

And how it's all going to hurt a lot worse than the friggin' IV needle, and for a lot longer.

"Hey, I've tried to call for three days."

I can't believe Scott has the audacity. But I just say, "I told my mom to tell you I wasn't home."

"I gathered."

"You weren't in economics, either."

"I rearranged my schedule."

He's quiet for a second. "I wanted to tell you I'm sorry. You have to believe me: I didn't mean to make you so sick. Or to hurt you at all. I love you, Jenna. I just—"

"Scott, you don't even want to know what I think about you right now." That I'm hurt. That I feel cheated and lied to. That all he ever really wanted was to get into my pants, and that when I made him wait too long, he figured he'd get in there one way or another.

That he couldn't possibly have ever loved me.

"Can't you forgive me? I know you love me too. Or at least you did."

I shove my homework aside and fiddle with the pencil cup on my desk. I don't know what to say to him. I wouldn't have to say anything to him if my parents had been home, because if his name had popped up on the caller ID downstairs, they'd have told him to leave me alone. And I wouldn't have answered if I'd seen his name on the ID.

But maybe it's good that I did. Maybe I need to get all this out.

"Jenna?"

"You know, I don't think you ever really loved me, Scott. I think you loved Bridget. And I think when that blew up, you decided to go for a girl who was her total opposite. Someone who isn't a prom queen, popular type. Someone like me. Because you knew I'd never cheat on you. I was a safety girlfriend for you, nothing more. Because if you really loved me, you wouldn't have done what you did."

"That's not it—"

"Maybe not." I swallow hard, then shove the pencil cup away. "Courtney's always told me I'm awful at reading people. But even if my Bridget theory is wrong, I know for a fact that you didn't love me. And I'm thinking I didn't know you as well as I thought. And that I couldn't possibly have loved you the way I thought I did, because the Scott I thought I loved wasn't capable of doing what you did, whether you meant to hurt me or not. I thought I could trust you. I thought you understood me, or at least that you wanted to *try* to understand me."

I hear him sigh. And I think he's actually crying. "I did. I still do. I just screwed it all up. Please, Jenna—"

"No, Scott. Just let me go."

I can hear him breathing on the other end of the line, and I know that I was 100 percent right not to have sex with him that night at the hotel. Even if we had, he would have done something like this eventually. Because the bottom line is that I can't trust him. I can *never* trust him.

He whispers good-bye and, with a click, he's gone.

I listen to the phone until the line starts to buzz, and then I put my head down on my desk and cry.

To: SuperMark@emailwizardry.net
From: JennaK@sfhs.edu
Subject: Update on everything

Hey, Mark. Sorry I haven't e-mailed lately. However, I have many updates:

1. I am coming to see you for spring break. Give me a call and we'll work out when I should fly down there, etc.

2. You do not need to worry about Scott and sex and all that. We broke up. So I won't leave you in suspense on that front anymore.

3. Have I told you lately that you're extremely cool? And that I need to listen to you more often?

Your adoring (though slow to write back) cousin, Jenna

To: JennaK@sfhs.edu
From: SuperMark@emailwizardry.net
Subject: RE: Update on everything

Hey yourself. Do NOT worry about not writing. And regarding your updates:

1. You passed up the class trip to Disney World, huh? (Betcha don't remember mentioning it to me forever ago, do you?) Anyway, I'm glad you're coming to see me instead.

2. You bet your ass you broke up. Your

mom told my parents what happened. That piece of you-know-what better never come within a hundred miles of me or I'll make sure he never walks again—or even thinks about sex. And, for the record, I'm really, really sorry it happened. You deserve way better, and I hope you're okay. (I know you'll be okay in the long term, but I mean okay in the short term. I worry about you.)

3. Of course I'm cool. I'm Super Mark, remember? And of course you should listen to me more often. Everyone should.

Always here for you, Mark

P.S. I have a friend I'd like you to meet. And no, he isn't the type to pressure you for sex. Yes, he's straight; yes, he's smart; and yes, he's good looking (or so my female friends tell me—much to my disgust—using words like "hottie" and "incredibly gorgeous" to describe him. Apparently they haven't taken a good look at me. . . .). And no, you don't have to go out with him. My guess is, you're not ready for all that, anyway. But it might be good for your ego to realize there are other guys out there, and that they're far better than what's-his-face, who will die if I see him first.

Epilogue

Sometimes, when I'm on the library steps, I still think about Scott Bannister and the day we came here on our college tour. The day he promised that we'd be spending this year together.

And even though at the time I thought it was the most romantic thing in the world, now I stand here and think about how happy I am that things didn't turn out that way. That he's living his life, doing his thing, and that I'm living mine.

What happened in the months after the roofie incident is a blur. For me, it's a blur by choice. I simply don't want to think about it too much. For everyone else, it's become the stuff of urban legend around South Framingham High School. Like the gossip that's spread in the halls after the popular kids' parties, where no one quite remembers who said what to whom. The kind of gossip I never thought would be about me.

Anne says that she's heard people talking about it—mostly the new freshmen and the sophomores—asking one another if they'd heard about the senior who gave his girlfriend the date rape drug last year, and that the girlfriend busted him to the police. Anne even told Courtney that one time she overheard one freshman tell another that the girlfriend died, but that the administration wants it kept quiet so no one will think there's a drug problem in the school.

And in a way, I guess I did die on that New Year's. Or part of me did. The part that thought I was bulletproof. The part that believed if I studied hard and followed all the rules and was nice to everyone, that nothing could hurt me. And the part that believed I could keep other people's problems from affecting me. That I could stand on my own two feet without help from anyone else.

I learned that those things aren't necessarily true. Being strong is important. But knowing who you can count on is equally important.

In the end, Scott got off with community service . . . well, and a mighty punishment from his mother, who was probably the only person more angry about the whole thing than I was. She convinced Scott's dad that the Jetta needed to be sold and the money donated to a drug awareness charity to teach Scott a lesson.

He's here somewhere. At Harvard.

It's not a surprise that he got in, really. I heard that he got in everywhere he applied. Even Brown, with that insane Walter Mondale essay. (That thing earned him a scholarship. Go figure.) But he was apparently telling me the truth when he said Harvard was his first-choice school, because I've seen him here a couple times.

Once, he was standing in line behind me in a bookstore. After I paid for my books, I made a beeline out of there without talking to him. The other time, he was with this really cute redhead, walking along the Charles River. After they passed me, it occurred to me that I should warn her. Like I wish Courtney had warned me.

If I see her with him again, I might.

But I'm not sure it'd be the right thing to do. I mean, I still wonder if he did what he did out of immaturity, or because he was still a little insecure after his whole blowup with Bridget over the Holliston Hottie. As stupid as it was, as dangerous and deceptive as it was, I don't think he was evil. Like all of us, he has shades of gray. And a hopeful part of me wants to believe that Scott learned his lesson, like I learned mine.

I know Courtney learned hers, too. We're still tight. Maybe tighter than ever, even though we don't see each other like we did in high school. She lives in one of the BU dorms, across the river from me. But sometimes on weekends I pack up my dirty clothes and take them over to her dad's apartment in Brookline. We spend the afternoon doing our laundry together and talking about our classes and all our new friends. It's really nice, since we both know we can share everything new that's happening in our lives and get a totally unbiased opinion about things. And it gives us a chance to get away from the dorms, away from all the drama.

I think we both had enough drama last year to keep us for the rest of our lives.

Sometimes Mat comes over too. He and Courtney are more in love than ever. And even though he's still a bit of a flirt—it's definitely a cultural thing, by the way—they seem so grown up when they're together that it scares me sometimes. Not because I think they're making a mistake or rushing things. It's actually the opposite: There's a peace and a maturity to their relationship that I just don't see in other couples.

It wouldn't surprise me if they get married after college. I know that's three years away, but sometimes you just have a gut feeling about these things.

When I mentioned it to Courtney once, she told me to stop trying to read people. But she blushed when she said it.

I think it's helping Courtney that she's in counseling too. After the shoplifting thing—which the police said they wouldn't even pursue, since the stores decided not to prosecute once she paid them back for the stolen merchandise—she started thinking that maybe all the college stuff and her parents' divorce had been getting to her more than she wanted to admit. She says now that though she didn't realize it at the time, somehow the double whammy of having her parents split and my getting into Harvard and having my future all mapped out sent her into a kind of tailspin. Like she didn't know what her life was about anymore, and she couldn't count on anything or anyone. It's probably more complicated than that—like Courtney says, I'm horrible with understanding people issues—but I think she knows she can count on me. And on Anne and her parents, too. Mostly, though, I think she's learning to count on herself.

Well, and Mateus the Great. Who truly is great.

Speaking of which, I haven't told Courtney and Mat about my new boyfriend yet. But I will. One of these weekends, when we're doing laundry.

His name is Ryan. I met him when I went to visit Mark at Georgetown over spring break last year, but we didn't start actually dating until the end of the summer, when I went down to DC to visit Mark again.

Ryan's at Georgetown on a track scholarship, but he's not the dumb jock type at all. He's an economics major, and he wants to go to law school after he graduates. He's a total straight-arrow type (which I love), plus he's funny and sweet and way beyond hot.

And he has Mark's seal of approval, which is reassuring (though I'll never admit that to Mark).

It's a long-distance thing, but for now, it works. Ryan's a sophomore, so he's a year older than I am, and I kind of like that.

I don't think I mentioned that Ryan is from the Boston area too. He graduated from Holliston High School, which is why Mark thought to hook us up. He knew we'd see each other on holidays and stuff like that, since Ryan's in Boston for Christmas and during the summers. We even have a few mutual friends, which is kind of cool.

But the funniest part of it all is that Ryan recently told me about this totally embarrassing thing that happened to him in high school. He hooked up with this girl from *my* high school during a track meet. Afterward, he found out that she had some superpopular jock boyfriend, and that the boyfriend ended up dumping her over the whole thing and going out with someone else just for revenge.

Ryan told me it's always bugged him—just a little bit. It wasn't like he knew the girl had a boyfriend or anything, but he felt kind of bad that her relationship ended because of him.

I told him to let it go. Not only are we all mistake-prone humans, we all have bad things happen to us that aren't of our own doing, and that what happened *totally* wasn't his own doing. I showed him the harmony necklace Courtney bought me, and told him I like it because it reminds me that we just have to learn from our mistakes—no matter what they are—and move on. Things will be better in the future.

What I didn't tell Ryan is that, for me, ending up—at least for now—with the guy Scott and I referred to as the Holliston Hottie and finding out that he's really a wonderful guy, someone who loves me for me, is pretty damned bizarre. But it's also what I consider the perfect kind of closure.

Author's Note

If you're skipping ahead and reading this before you've read the book, be warned: I'm about to give away some key parts of the plot. If you hate having stories spoiled, come back to this later.

What happens to Jenna in *Sticky Fingers,* unfortunately, is becoming more common. Date rape drugs—the most common are Rohypnol (roofies), gamma hydroxy butyrate (GHB), and ketamine hydrochloride—are fairly easy to obtain. When dropped into a drink, they work to render the victim incapable of controlling her behavior as she normally would. She might appear intoxicated, as Jenna did, or confused and tired. Therefore, it's easy for a sexual predator to coax a drugged victim away from safety. Rapes can be committed in which the victim is oblivious to the assault. The drug can cause one to lose all memory of the event or leave the victim with only a vague recollection of something bad happening. In some cases, these drugs have even killed.

What makes these drugs so attractive to sexual predators is that they're difficult to detect—they're odorless, tasteless, and usually colorless. They take effect in a matter of minutes and work even in water. An attacker can drop the drug into a drink with a flick of the wrist, then watch from across the room as the victim becomes disoriented, and approach after the drug takes effect. These attackers also know that date rape drugs aren't picked up on standard toxicology tests, and that they leave the victim's bloodstream and urine in eight to seventy-two hours—at the most. In other words, in order to know what's happened, a victim must (1) suspect he or she has been drugged; (2) go to the police or, better yet, to the hospital; and (3) ask that the doctor perform specific tests for this group of drugs.

Fortunately there are several things you can do to protect yourself and your friends from these kinds of attacks:

1) Never accept open drinks from anyone you don't know or trust completely. This includes drinks in a glass.

2) If you're at a party or in a public place like a movie theater, take your drink directly from the person who prepares it. Watch while it's being prepared. If lids are available, put one on your drink immediately.

3) Never drink from open punch bowls and pitchers or take pre-poured glasses from a table.

4) Never leave your drink unattended on a table or turn your back while you have a conversation. If you can, finish your drink before you go dance or go to the restroom; otherwise, take the drink with you.

5) If you or a friend start to feel sick, disoriented, or "high" after consuming a drink, leave immediately with someone you trust and get medical attention.

6) If you still worry about falling victim to an attacker

in this way, consider some of the products on the market that test drinks for the presence of date rape drugs. One site offering coasters and test strips that do this is www.drinksafetech.com.

For more information, you can do a Web search for any of the date rape drugs by name. You may also wish to visit www.health.org or www.nih.gov (search these government sites for the term "date rape drug"). Knowledge is the key to prevention.